Bethany's
New Reality

Rachel John

ISBN: 1530895359
ISBN-13: 978-1530895359

ACKNOWLEDGMENTS

I'm always thankful for my awesome husband who encourages me to enjoy the creative side of life. I'd also like to thank my critique partners, Melanie D. Snitker, Franky A. Brown, Victorine E. Lieske, and Crystal Walton, my beta readers Robin Cranney and K.J. Watters, and my proofreader, Faith Blum.

CHAPTER 1

The morning crew trickled out of their after-the-show meeting and Jeffy's eyes lit up when he spotted me. He came over to the water cooler and leaned on it as I pretended to fill up my bottle for the fourth time. He was blocking my view of the door, so I took a step back and leaned against the wall, drinking slowly. I needed Mr. Langley in my line of sight.

"Hey, lady." Jeffy grinned at me and raised an eyebrow seductively.

Oh, Jeffy. You are just one more reason I have to get out of here.

"Bethany," Mr. Langley called out. "Come in, I want to talk to you."

Wow, loitering outside my boss's office worked. I gave Jeffy a little wave and went into Mr. Langley's tiny kingdom. Since three radio stations shared the building, every space was precious. At least my boss had the luxury of a window.

I walked in, feigning surprise. This morning, when I'd dropped my request for a month off, I didn't anticipate the gnawing anxiety that would follow me the rest of the day. A medical emergency or a dying relative was a respectable reason to ask for time off. Needing time to date gorgeous men on TV, not so much. If I was going to get laughed out of his office, I didn't want to wait forever, replaying worse and worse versions of it in my head.

Six months ago I'd auditioned for a new dating reality show, *Real Love*. I'd just broken up with my boyfriend, Todd, and it was part of a late night internet search to distract me from my misery.

I'd filled out the forms, laughing at the thought of how I looked at that very moment, downing pints of ice cream, un-showered, unhinged, and dressed in green sweats as comfortable as they were hideous.

Getting chosen for the show never crossed my mind. Normally, I am decently attractive and fun. But you forget all that when you date someone like Todd. Self-absorbed jerk. And I didn't see it until it was too late, until after he'd sucked all the self-esteem out of me. I told myself all the follow up calls and questionnaires and background checks were a way to feed my ego until I got eliminated from the horde of women desperate for love or public attention or both. Now they were ready to fly me out to Los Angeles to be on their show. It was flattering, and surreal, and I was still a little bit in denial.

But losing my job? That was a real possibility. I liked working here, but I'd promised myself I'd quit if I didn't get the time off. The thought gave me a stomach ache. I'm usually too practical to be voluntarily unemployed.

Mr. Langley motioned for me to sit down. I sat in the chair opposite his desk and tried not to let my gaze wander around the room. Mr. Langley loved anti-motivational posters and had them all over the walls. My personal favorite was the one that said, 'BELIEVE IN YOURSELF: Because the rest of us think you're an idiot.'

"I saw your request this morning for a month off, and I'm approving it."

No way! My mouth dropped open and I quickly shut it and tried to think up a response. "Thank you so much, I…"

"Stop gushing and let's talk about this," Mr. Langley interrupted. "I called the producers of this dating show, *Real Love*, and told them if I was giving you a month off, I wanted you on our radio station, giving us the inside dish after you get back. They agreed to a cross promotional deal. This could create a huge ratings bump for us."

He drummed on his desk with excited energy. "Bethany, this could be big for us. This show's been bought by NBC. I need you to really get noticed, fall in love, break some hearts. Just stay there as long as possible. You can go back to your desk eventually, but first we are going to milk this for all its worth."

"Yes, Mr. Langley. You can count on me." I nodded with

assurance, but inside I was a frazzled mess. Why didn't I think this through? I worked behind radio, not on the radio. And I liked it that way. I should have known Mr. Langley would turn this into a marketing bit. He forced Patty to make a commercial about her stomach stapling surgery last year.

"Fantastic. I need you to turn over your unfinished ads to Patty before you leave and we'll hope she doesn't screw anything up while you're gone. Give your VIP clients to me." Mr. Langley stood, letting me know the meeting was over.

On the walk back to my desk, my emotions somersaulted from elation to complete terror. I'd won the dating lottery, and even though most of the girls who went on these shows went home crying, like everyone else, I hinged all my hopes on the chance it might be different for me. *And Mr. Langley can't wait for you to jump into this so the DJs can laugh about it.* My silly adventure had turned into an assignment.

***

I spent the rest of the week tying up loose ends at work and packing and organizing at home. With my fridge clean, landlord paid, and mail on hold, it felt like I was moving forward and not paralyzed with fear.

I'd had crazy adventures before, but always with a friend along, someone fearless who could laugh off my worries and help me relax and have fun. This would be different. I'd be all alone, walking into a situation I had no control over. And if I ended up humiliating myself, it wouldn't become an inside joke, it would be on entertainment news. I almost called and backed out, but the thought that I'd never get this chance again kept me from doing it. My nails were nubs by the end of the week and I went to get a last-minute manicure the night before I had to leave for California.

A phone call from Mom woke me the next morning.

"You didn't have to call." But I knew Mom would, even from Jamaica where she and Steve were on vacation.

"I wanted to say goodbye before you left today. I put it in my calendar."

Of course she did. Mom put everything in her calendar. She probably had my monthly cycle tracked in there.

"So, how is married life?" I asked.

"Amazing."

"Is Steve having fun?"

"He's not much of a beachgoer, but he loves the afternoon naps and the buffet."

"Of course he does."

"Dear, about this show..."

I let out a big sigh. I couldn't help myself.

"Now hear me out," Mom said.

"Go ahead."

"Promise me two things. Two things, my dear. One, that you will not embarrass yourself. And two, that you will not, under any circumstances, get engaged, or even, well, you know. Shows like this pressure people into bad decisions. Love takes time, I certainly should know. After your father died I never thought I'd remarry. And then when Steve came along, it took some time for him to convince me to even go on a first date. And even then, I only agreed to meet for coffee."

"I know, Mom," I answered, trying to cut her off. She loved to tell this story and it could drag on for hours or go into avenues I'd rather not visit with my mother. "I promise not to get engaged or shame you or myself. Satisfied?"

"I guess." She sighed. "I can't help worrying about you."

"I know. I love you. I'll call you when I get my phone back. I won't have access to it as part of my non-disclosure agreement."

"Are you sure you want to do this?"

"Bye, Mom."

"Don't forget to unplug your appliances."

"Love you, Mom."

"Bye, sweetheart. Love you, too."

I hung up and rolled out of bed before I gave into the temptation to fall back asleep. There was so much to do. First thing was to check the mirror. I'd passed puberty long ago, but occasionally a monster zit would show up right before something majorly important. The kind that laughs in the face of makeup and reminds you what it is to be human.

Thank heavens, a clear face. One small miracle. I tried not to stare while I brushed my teeth. No need to analyze myself through the eyes of TV viewers. I'm not normally insecure. I'm a nice looking brunette. I can turn heads. But the thought of millions of viewers judging my looks terrified me.

Get it together, Bethany. This is for fun. This is an adventure. I'm adventurous. With my new mantra repeating in my head, I continued my morning routine.

The doorbell rang as I was stepping out of the shower. Throwing on a bathrobe, I ran downstairs to let Katelyn in, my ride to the airport. My best friend looked so cute with her round belly popping out from her sundress. Only Katelyn could rock pregnancy like a supermodel. She took off her sunglasses and perched them on her blonde head.

"That's not very much luggage," she said, pointing at my little green suitcase in the corner.

"They're providing wardrobe. I'm just bringing extras, like workout clothes and pajamas."

"Any lingerie?"

"I'm not you," I answered, sticking out my tongue. I sat down across from her at the table and poured myself a bowl of cereal. "Want some?"

Katelyn grinned and let me fill up a bowl of Cap'n Crunch for her. She never passed up snacking opportunities these days.

"And you really want to do this?" she asked through a mouthful of cereal.

"You sound like my mother."

Katelyn grinned. "Your mom's a smart lady. She met Steve at church."

I raised an eyebrow. "This is coming from the woman who met her husband at a wet T-shirt contest?"

Katelyn made a face. "You were there too. I will disown you and call you a liar if you ever tell my parents I met Doug there. They think we met on a blind date."

"Just don't judge me if I want to try this. If it doesn't work out, then maybe I'll write a tell-all book and make millions."

"Speaking of...they are paying you to go on this thing aren't they?"

"Yes, but I'm not supposed to say how much. They refer to it as compensation for time and travel. But it's really a paid vacation."

Katelyn laughed. "You are trying so hard to be cynical about this."

"I'm a realist. A realist going on a reality show to do some pretend dating. You're right. I shouldn't do this. Do you think it's because I'm turning thirty? Is this a midlife crisis?"

"Thirty is too young for a midlife crisis." Katelyn touched my damp hair. "Let's go make you presentable and then you can freak out during the flight. And if you call and say you're coming home tonight I'll drive back to the airport and pick you up. No questions asked."

"Really?"

"Bethany, you got this. Honestly, I'd be a little more worried if you were a drinker. You know they're going to try to booze you up for the camera."

"I'll be such a disappointment. Passed out on the couch after one glass of wine." I stood up and threw our paper bowls in the trash and then pulled the bag out to take with me when we left.

Katelyn took over picking an outfit, doing my hair and applying my makeup. I was happy to let her. If I could bring her along as my personal hair and makeup artist I would. However, I didn't think the show would want someone giving birth on set.

"Hey," I reached up and touched her hand. "Don't have the little guy until I get back, okay?"

Katelyn looked down at me and rolled her eyes. "I'll send him a memo."

She seemed thoughtful as she brushed out my dark hair, looking for stray pieces to straighten. "Bethany, we've done so many crazy things together. But I can't be wild and crazy anymore. I'm glad you're doing this reality show. You need an adventure that's for you."

I nodded. It was a good pep talk. And I needed one. I felt like I was going into shock. She was making me camera-ready. My face glowed. My hair was sleek and smooth. But would I be able to hide the insecurities and doubts underneath all that? Highly doubtful.

We didn't talk about the reality show as we drove to the airport. I didn't want to hash it out again. I just wanted to get it over with before I chickened out. Kind of like the time we went bungee jumping.

CHAPTER 2

It wasn't until I saw a driver holding up a sign saying 'Bethany Parks' that I almost changed my mind. I let him stand there for several minutes before I finally got the nerve to present myself.

My attempts to be chatty didn't work. Frank, the driver, was not familiar with the workings of the show and gruffly told me he wasn't supposed to say anything about it anyway. I finally gave up asking him questions and sat in the back of the sedan on my way to what I assumed would be a secluded resort. Instead, we traveled farther and farther from the city, into the high desert suburbs.

I had dozed off, but jerked awake when the sedan pulled to a stop in front of a rundown apartment complex with a postage-stamp sized pool. *What is this?* There was little time to question it. My door opened and I was accosted by an enthusiastic man with a bristly mustache and a finger-crushing handshake. He wore a dark blazer over a tight aqua T-shirt and loafers without socks.

"I'm Greg. You must be Bethany. We are so excited you're here, but we're behind schedule, so if you would please come with me..." He looked me up and down and clapped his hands together. "Good, no logos. Solid colors. Hair looks good."

Greg explained to Frank where to drop my bag and then I followed Greg into a small conference room crammed with cameras and crewmembers. There were cords taped to the floor everywhere. He led me to a neat semi-circle of chairs and I took the last one.

"Make yourself comfortable. We'll be getting started in a few minutes."

A girl came around doing a quick makeup and hair check and attached a tiny microphone to my shirt. I didn't want to give up my purse, but it couldn't be in the shot, so off it went into a pile of purses from all the other contestants. She also pinned a nametag on me. It seemed tacky for a reality show, but useful as I took a quick survey of my competition and could tie names to faces…although I wasn't sure I wanted to call them competition yet. We hadn't exactly been told how all of this would work.

Good thing I'd let Katelyn pick my clothes. Apparently I was going on camera for the first time just as I was. They wanted to start right away? I took a deep breath and tried to keep my head from swiveling back and forth. One thing at a time.

There were seven of us. Beside me was a pretty Asian girl with thick, black hair that swept down her back. Her nametag read Michelle. Gretchen sat on the other side of her. She was super tan, with golden blonde hair and dark brown eyes. She looked a bit older than me, but the rest of the women looked younger. Jada sat next to her. She was a gorgeous black woman with long legs and a severe stare. She didn't seem very impressed with the show so far and I couldn't blame her. My instincts were crying out 'low budget!' and I wondered if this thing would even end up on the air.

"Two minute warning, people," the director called out. "Ladies, sit up and cross your ankles. Legs together, make it classy."

An assistant dropped a thick envelope on my lap, but as I began to open it the director started yelling again. "No one open your packets yet. We'll do it on camera. Someone pull those calla lilies out of the flower arrangement. They're blocking the cameras. Are we ready, Greg?"

Greg gave him two enthusiastic thumbs up. He turned a blindingly bright smile on us and then pursed his lips together like he was trying to hold back a flood of emotion. "Ladies, before we get started, I want to introduce myself and explain my role. I am Greg Lee, your host. I will be with you through the duration of the show and on camera with you. Any questions or concerns go through me, but the real boss is Dave Maxwell, your director back there. A quick round of applause for the genius behind the show. Thank you, Dave."

He started clapping so we had no choice but to follow his example and give a hesitant round of applause for our director.

Dave looked no more than twenty-five and wore grungy sweatpants, yet had a commanding presence that made everyone around him scurry to obey.

Dave nodded in acknowledgement, watching from behind one of the cameras and signaling to the various cameramen in the room. Greg continued on with more introductions, often breaking out into a big smile that was both reassuring and creepy all at the same time. If you could morph Dr. Phil and Ryan Seacrest, you would have a picture of Greg. He was introducing the cameramen, as if any of us cared, when I heard Michelle murmur, "Enough of this, when do we meet the men?" She grinned at me and I smiled back, rolling my eyes.

"So," Greg clapped his hands together. "We are going to get started in a moment and read from the packets. You'll learn all the rules, how the show will work and a little bit about the men you'll be dating. We'll have you take turns reading. Act natural and relaxed. We want genuine reactions, but try to look at each other or me and not directly up at the cameras. Don't be nervous, we'll fix everything in editing and splice it with the reactions from the men. They were filmed yesterday. So who's ready to make some great TV?"

We all clapped, some of us in impatience and others in excitement. A girl across from me named Sylvie looked like she was ready to pop out of her chair. Her curly black hair bounced on her shoulders like she'd walked out of a Pantene commercial. She had flawless ivory skin and a sweetheart-shaped face.

"Why don't we start with you, Sylvie?" Greg gave her a wink and she giggled nervously. "Everyone open their packets now and Sylvie, you read first."

"Sure, Greg." Her excitement waned a little as her eyes skimmed down the page. I opened my packet and read along with her, quickly realizing why she'd lost her smile.

"Welcome to the most progressive and realistic dating show ever created," she began. "We are bringing the 'real' back to reality TV. In the next few hours you will discover that your accommodations are more college dorm than sprawling mansion. There are no maids or wait staff, so you might want to make your bed and wash your own dishes. America will be watching after all." Sylvie dropped her packet back into her lap and stared at Greg. "Is this a joke?"

Greg gave her a sympathetic smile and motioned to Michelle, the Asian girl next to me with the long dark hair. "Please read for us next."

Michelle frowned and picked up her packet. "On this show there are seven men and seven women. This is not the dating apocalypse where only one man is left on earth and twenty-five women throw themselves at his feet. There will be no rose ceremonies, limos or luxury trips. In fact, you probably noticed we gave you nametags to wear. Real men struggle to remember women's names, even if they like you. Please keep your nametag on for the rest of the day."

Ugh, what did I get myself into? They let us think this would be luxurious, fun, and romantic, all so they could have this gotcha moment. I pictured the editor in my mind, cutting from our group to the men, just as clueless, reading the rules and wondering how to get out of this. My mind started reviewing all the paperwork I'd already signed. The title of the show, *Real Love*, was starting to make more sense.

The overly-tan blonde, Gretchen, tried to read next, but she kept pausing to read ahead silently and Greg finally gave up and asked Jada to read instead.

"Most of you haven't worn eveningwear since high school prom, so you won't find any formal dresses in your wardrobe. You live life in regular clothes and you'll date in them. We want you to look beyond appearances to see the person within." Jada looked up with an irritated face. "So you assumed I'm a jeans and T-shirt girl?" She leaned back and crossed her legs as she gave her miniskirt a tug to cover her derriere and then glared at Dave. "I'll sit how I want," she muttered. "No limos, no dresses."

She said something that would have to be bleeped and then finally went silent when Greg cleared his throat and asked a woman named Anna to read next. Anna fidgeted with her white-blonde hair, tucking it behind an ear as she began.

"In the real dating world, your new boyfriend is someone's old boyfriend. Everyone has a past. So you seven ladies will be choosing from each other's seven exes. You read that right. Each one of you has an ex-boyfriend in the group of men you'll be dating." Anna's blue eyes went wide and she let out a tiny scream.

There was a collective gasp and my body went numb. Did that mean Todd was here? I couldn't think of anyone else from my past they could bring. I would have to face him on national TV while he dated the other contestants. Could they possibly have recruited us without letting any of us know we'd all be here together? Perhaps Director Dave was an evil genius.

I snuck a glance at Michelle and saw a similar gamut of emotions running across her face.

With some prodding from Greg, Anna continued. "Rest assured, extensive background checks have been done on everyone and none of the men you will meet today are married or have a criminal record. Your fellow contestants can give you more information on the gentlemen you are soon to meet."

The room exploded in yelling and in one case sobbing. I looked over and saw the director grinning. He was loving this. Our host, Greg, tried to look sympathetic and rushed to calm us all down.

"I am not okay with this!" a tiny redhead named Holly wailed. "When you asked us about our past relationships you said it was part of our background check." Greg tried to put an arm around her shoulder but she pushed him off and headed to the women's bathroom, slamming the door behind her.

Gretchen and Sylvie scooted over to us. Solidarity among us women who weren't hysterical, I guess. They had a pad of paper out and seemed to be comparing notes on possible exes. At the moment, I didn't give a hoot who would be on this show. I wasn't about to lock myself in a bathroom, but there was a good possibility I'd be looking for an escape route if things didn't turn around soon.

"They probably recruited Tyson," Gretchen said, flipping her thick blonde hair over her shoulder. "He's the type to go on a show like this. But I've dated a lot." She shrugged. "It could be anyone."

I glanced down at their list.

Sylvie - Eddie (personal trainer - not ready for a serious relationship)

Gretchen - Tyson? (immature)

"How old is he, Gretchen?"

"Twenty-four. No wait, his birthday was in Mar—" She stopped talking to listen to Anna ranting to Jada.

"I was engaged last year, but I broke it off because he was so unhappy. I can't believe this is happening!" Anna burst into tears again. We'd only been filming for ten minutes and the waterworks were already flowing. I felt bad for her, but I also wanted her to get it together for all womankind.

Sylvie wrote down: *Anna - was engaged, ex sounds promising*

"Sylvie!" Gretchen protested.

Sylvie shrugged. "I don't know about you, but I came here to find a man. Take your own notes if you don't like it."

"What about you?" It took me a second to realize they were looking at me. "Who's your ex?"

I glanced at the cameraman above us, even though I was supposed to pretend he wasn't there. "I think they'll have Todd here. We couldn't do the long distance thing."

The girls nodded in understanding, not questioning me further. What I'd said was true, if a bit misleading. More like he created a long-distance problem so he could break up with me, but they didn't need to know that.

Bethany - Todd (long-distance)

They interrogated the rest of us to finish out the list.

Michelle - Patrick? (College boyfriend - practical joke gone wrong)

Jada -- Marco (on again, off again)

"What about Holly?"

"Who?"

"The girl in the bathroom."

"Who's your ex, Holly?" Sylvie yelled at the bathroom door.

"Go away!" Holly answered back. "I'm not doing this show. This is not what I signed up for. You hear me Greg with the ugly loafers?"

There was a boom mike operator right at the bathroom door and I tried not to laugh. What kind of show was this?

Sylvie smiled and made a note: *Holly - Not over him*

"Can she quit?" Michelle asked.

Gretchen whipped through the pages and nodded. "Yes. But it says anyone who chooses to leave before they're voted off will forfeit the money and pay their way home. Harsh." She skimmed down further and read, "The show will run for eight episodes, with the possibility of elimination at the end of every episode. Each episode will take approximately three days to film." Her eyes glanced over the next few paragraphs and then she looked at us and frowned. "I guess we vote for the guy we're most interested in, and the guys do the same for us. Anyone with zero votes gets eliminated."

"What? Hand me that." Sylvie snatched the packet out of Gretchen's hands and started reading it for herself. "How humiliating. Basically, if none of the guys are interested in you, you go home, and everyone knows what a big loser you are."

Greg interrupted. "Ladies, voting is a necessary and positive part of your journey. Think about it. If one of the men does not capture the interest of any of you, do you still want him on the show?" He didn't wait for us to answer. "You are here to find true love. The voting process is an important and necessary part of your journey."

His intrusion felt rude, which was stupid considering the three cameras zoomed in to capture every angle. Obviously, nothing said aloud was private. I knew a lot of his flowery crap was for the cameras, but it made it impossible for me to take him seriously. Unfortunately, I had more questions and he was the one with the answers.

"Who will see our votes?" I asked.

"Everyone!" Greg smiled brightly as he said it, as if it was the most wonderful thing in the world. "Dave wants an open and vibrant dialogue. We would ask you ladies to keep your votes secret until elimination night, but then you are free to express your feelings openly."

"Then how many of us are making it to the final episode?" Gretchen asked.

Greg shrugged. "It will depend on the votes. If you fall in love and your love is returned, then you'll make it through each and every episode. America will see your whole journey unfold."

I was getting a bit tired of the word journey, and starting to wonder when our journey would involve food. I hadn't eaten anything substantial since breakfast. However, we hadn't discussed the real problem yet, why the show had to involve our exes.

Greg tried to spin it in a positive light. "Think of all the inside information you'll have on these fellows. These are good men. I've sat down and talked to each one of them. They've been bruised on the road to love, but now they are ready for a serious, committed relationship and they come with the best intentions, just like you."

"So when do we meet these good men and their serious

intentions?" Jada asked, not trying to hide the sarcasm.

"Yes, when do we see them?" Gretchen asked.

Dave interrupted with an announcement. "That was great ladies, but we need to get back in our chairs and do it a few more times before we do any introducing."

The makeup artists made the rounds again to fix any hairs out of place and get eye makeup under control for those who had been crying. An assistant passed around water bottles and then gathered them up again so they wouldn't be in any of the shots. Greg and Dave tried again to coax Holly out of the bathroom. They had the whole good cop/bad cop thing going. After a few promises about perks and extra air time, and threats about breach of contract, she finally came out and subjected herself to a makeup redo.

She avoided looking at any of us and I tried to stop staring. It was hard to know where to look or what expression to try to put on my face. Was I supposed to smile through all of this? Because what I was probably projecting was grim shock, thinly-veiled disgust, and embarrassment. *Real attractive, Bethany.*

I'd been cast in a nightmare version of *Seven Brides for Seven Brothers*. I remembered the movie. Those brides had a bad case of Stockholm syndrome. *But if a hot lumberjack stole you for the winter, you'd get over it.*

Greg jolted me out of my musings. "Bethany, I need you to read. Pick the paragraph that bothers you the most. Give us some feeling."

I glanced down at my packet and decided to read the part where our exes were the other contestants. It wasn't hard to give them the emotional reaction they were looking for. *They want us to look mad.* That thought only ticked me off more.

It took another two hours for Dave to be satisfied, but they finally let us out of our chairs and made an announcement. "Barbeque on the front lawn in forty minutes. If you want to meet the guys you should go get ready. A wardrobe change is mandatory. Your room assignments are at the end of the packet. Your bags are already up there. Hair, makeup, and wardrobe must be approved before leaving the building. And don't forget your nametag!"

CHAPTER 3

My room assignment was with Michelle in apartment four. We headed up the stairs together and walked into our temporary home. A cameraman stood in front to catch our reactions. I took in the small sitting area, a kitchenette, and a tiny bedroom with matching twin beds. Grayish-blue carpeting looked like a leftover from a bygone era.

I wanted to glance back at the cameraman, but forced myself to look at Michelle instead. "What is this place?"

Michelle frowned. "I don't know, but I don't think it's been refurbished since 1979." She used two fingers to peel back an ugly floral bedspread from one of the twin beds and threw it on the floor.

I stalked over to inspect the closet, no longer excited they were providing wardrobe. A scream from next door seemed to confirm my fears. Michelle pushed passed me and flipped on the closet light.

"I knew it! Bethany, look at this horror show."

I peeked in and gasped. Mom jeans, knitted sweaters, polyester turtlenecks, and peasant skirts. Michelle bent down and sniffed one of the sweaters. "At least they don't smell as bad as they look. It's like a thrift store in here, one that's already been picked over by people with taste."

"Do we have to wear these?" I asked.

"Afraid so." Michelle turned to the cameraman and boom mike operator. "Okay, out. You got our reactions, now we have some trying on to do." She followed them to the front door and slammed it behind them. "Gahhh!" she screamed.

I ran to the front room, looking around for a rat, or a roach, or a hairy sweater. "What? What is it?"

Michelle let out a sigh. "Nothing, I needed to scream. Can I break something? Do you think they'd miss that lamp?"

I laughed. "They were so secretive about the details. Now I know why. I should have listened to my mom."

"But you're going to be on TV," Michelle said, teasing.

"In mom jeans, standing next to my ex-boyfriend." We stared at each other for a moment and then burst out laughing.

After several try-ons, Michelle chose an ivory peasant skirt and a maroon sweater. I finally settled on a short sleeve turtleneck with wide black and white stripes and overly-flared jeans with artificial whiskers at the hips.

We left our room to meet up with the other women on the stairway. They were dressed just as frumpy, but we were all too embarrassed to laugh at each other. On the director's signal, we walked down to the courtyard where the men were standing around anticipating our arrival. A handful of cameramen stood in the background to capture our first meeting from every angle.

Jada stopped in her tracks and pointed to a muscled Mario Lopez look-alike in a hideous Hawaiian print button-down. "I changed my mind. I'm not over my ex. If any of you make a move on him, I'll cut you." She smiled back at us and we laughed nervously, afraid she was only half joking. She walked over and claimed his arm. He smiled at her and whispered in her ear. When she glanced back at us we all pretended not to be watching.

"Well that leaves six of them." Sylvie gave a disappointed sigh.

"Which one's yours?" Michelle whispered.

I nodded my head in Todd's direction. "He let his hair grow out. I don't like it."

Brown wavy hair grazed his chin. Paired with his red and black plaid shirt and manpris, he looked like a 1990s grunger. Not that I could blame him for the wardrobe. I had a chance to study him because he didn't even glance in my direction. He was too busy looking at Gretchen, and she was staring longingly at a guy with slicked-back blond hair and dimples. His nametag said 'Eddie.' The personal trainer, I remembered. Sylvie's ex. Sylvie's eyes narrowed as she watched Gretchen and Eddie walk up to each other and introduce themselves. They were like a walking advertisement for tanning cream and unbridled lust.

I grabbed Michelle's arm before she could leave my side. "Director Dave is an evil genius."

"Director Dave?"

"That's what I call him in my head. But look, he's guaranteed catfights from the very beginning by forcing our exes on us. This is like a real-life soap opera—only with bad clothes. Look at Sylvie. She can't decide if she wants to play it cool or throw herself between Eddie and Gretchen."

"That's so wrong."

"And yet, I'd watch this. If it was on TV."

Michelle nodded and nudged me forward. "Come on then. Let's get on TV."

We walked over to the two guys sitting at a picnic table covered in food. My need to eat propelled me forward.

They looked up and smiled at our approach. "Hello ladies. I'm Tyson and this is Max." Tyson patted the spot next to him so I sat down. He was cute and young, probably not even twenty-five. Michelle sat down next to Max, a wiry guy with dark curly hair, and he visibly stiffened in nervousness.

"She won't bite," I teased.

Michelle winked at him. "Well I won't if you feed me. Are those ribs?" Max handed Michelle a plate and she peeked under one of the foil-covered platters at the end of the table. The smell of barbeque sauce filled the air. Another platter was piled high with corn on the cob. There were a couple bags of nacho-flavored chips and Tyson ripped one open.

It wasn't until we'd filled up our plates and I'd taken my first bite that I thought to ask, "Where are the napkins?"

Tyson looked up from licking his barbeque fingers and smiled at me. "Don't need 'em."

Michelle rolled her eyes. "Seriously, I need a napkin." She held up her orange chip fingers and a camera man zoomed in closer.

Tyson noticed the camera and pulled off his oversized gray polo. "I'll donate this to a good cause." Clearly he'd been looking for an invitation to get out of the horrible shirt and show off his ripped abs.

I pictured the evil, glittering eyes of Director Dave as he thought up this stupid scenario and grabbed the proffered shirt. "If you offer your chest next, I am not wiping my hands on it."

"Sweetheart, this is a family show," Tyson warned, winking at me.

My face grew hot and I vowed to be more careful with my mouth. *Sorry Mom.*

"Can I borrow that shirt when you're done?" a male voice asked. I turned to my left and stared right into the ocean grey-blue eyes of the guy next to me. He must have sat down while I was whining about napkins.

"Hi, I'm Carter Allred."

I didn't remember his name from the list and blurted out, "Who's your ex?" before I thought better of it.

His smile faltered a little. "Holly."

"Oh." Crazy bathroom girl. I should have known. Then I remembered my manners. "I'm Bethany Parks. Nice to meet you." I handed him Tyson's shirt and he wiped barbeque sauce from his fingers. I tried not to stare, but I couldn't help myself. He had close-cropped blond curls and the little cleft in his chin. I was too smart to believe in love at first sight, but I did believe in instant attraction. I'd have to be careful.

After a splash behind us, we turned and saw Jada and her not ex-boyfriend Marco in the pool in their underwear. The cameras gravitated over in their direction and Carter leaned over as soon the boom mike lurking over our heads left.

"What's a nice girl like you doing on a show like this?" he asked.

I gazed into his eyes, trying to see if he was baiting me for a flirty response like, 'who says I'm a nice girl,' but he seemed genuinely concerned.

"Do you know something I don't?" I asked. A cameraman was making his way back to us and I knew we only had about thirty seconds.

Carter frowned. "This show is going to be all about making us look stupid. They let some of us eat before you girls came down and then started interviewing us about our exes. I watched Todd, your ex, doing an interview with a corn kernel stuck in his teeth. I was about to interrupt, but then I heard what he was saying about you."

What had Todd said about me? I would have to interrogate Carter later because the cameraman was back. Carter cleared his throat, reminding me I should stop frowning.

"Do you want to go for a walk?" he asked.

Before I could respond, an arm reached between us and dragged Carter from his seat. Holly shrieked at the top of her lungs. "I hate you, Carter! How could you do this to me?"

Carter put his arms around her and tried to shush her, moving her away from the table. For a petite girl, she was awfully strong. I shielded my face and went back to concentrating on my food. Even if this was the only episode I was on, it might be too much.

Carter finally managed to get Holly to stop screaming about how she'd totally moved on and didn't need him to keep showing up in her life.

He kept reassuring her, "Holly, I didn't know you would be here. I didn't know."

Holly nodded and wiped her eyes and Carter held her while she cried.

Tyson nudged me. "Wow. They are really milking it for the cameras."

"You think it's an act?"

Tyson shrugged. "Gretchen hasn't even looked at me. You don't see her over here dragging me out of my seat. She could care less that we dated once. But then, she's not dying to be on camera like that Holly chick."

I looked at Carter and Holly again, wondering if I'd ever be able to take anything at face value. "Why are you here?" I asked Tyson.

He shrugged. "Got recruited. I didn't know it was because of Gretchen. I thought they liked my impressive guns." He flexed and I couldn't help laughing. I wasn't sure if he was an egomaniac or a goof. Maybe both.

"What about this true reality format, with the frumpy clothes and crappy apartment?"

"It's stupid, but then, it's reality TV. It's supposed to be stupid." He purposely smirked up at the camera as he said it. Then he touched my arm. "Don't leave yet," he whispered. "I know you want to. I can see it in your face. Stick around for a while and let's see how this pans out."

I looked into his eyes and I swear we had a moment. Not a sparks flying kind of moment, more like an instant bond, like I knew we were going to be friends, allies in this. And I knew I'd need an ally to get through the next few weeks. I nodded. "Okay, I won't go yet."

CHAPTER 4

Greg came over and stole me away for an interview. Gretchen had just finished and I motioned for her to check my teeth, thinking of Todd. She gave me a thumbs up and I sat down on the bench so they could get my microphone attached and smooth my hair.

Greg began with, "Tell us a little about yourself, Bethany."

I tried to think of something interesting and funny to say and completely blanked. Maybe it was all the chaos in the background. Jada streaked by in her underwear, followed by Marco. Todd was not so casually standing next to the cameraman. He'd finally noticed me, if only so he could spy on my interview.

Greg made a rolling motion with his hand. "Don't be nervous. We'll fix everything in editing."

That didn't make me feel better. They could make me any version of me they wanted to in editing.

"I'm Bethany...as you can see by my nametag."

Greg gave an exaggerated laugh and I inwardly cringed.

"I'm twenty-nine and I'm a radio station marketing specialist." Shoot, all the stuff that would already be on the bottom of the screen under my face when they aired this. At least I was employed so they didn't have to make up a career for me. I'd heard some of these shows did that. Would they have to shorten Radio Marketing Specialist? I knew my boss would love an on-air plug. Was there a casual way to mention KYLM Country Radio in a conversation? I looked at Greg and realized he was starting to question my sanity. How long had my thoughts wandered?

Tyson scooted in next to me on the bench and put his arm around me. "This is Bethany. She likes barbeque and shirtless men."

I gave him a friendly nudge and then theatrically pushed him off the bench. "Thank you, Tyson, but this is *my* interview." It was the boost of confidence I needed.

"I love to golf, but I hate golf clothes. If it was up to me I'd golf barefoot in a ratty T-shirt and jeans. I'm a bargain shopper, but I love designer handbags. That's my one splurge. I'm a terrible cook, but I love to make dessert. I have a serious sweet tooth."

Greg looked down at his notes. "What are you looking for in a man?"

I resisted the urge to roll my eyes. "I want what everyone wants. Someone honest, funny, loyal, and I want to find him attractive."

"What about your ex, Todd?"

My back stiffened, but I forced myself to smile. "Are you asking if he has those qualities?"

Greg loved this answer. "Yes. What qualities does Todd have, and what did he lack for you?"

"Todd was all those things."

"Was?"

"Greg," I warned. "You're digging."

He shrugged. "Give me a shovel."

He wanted all the gooey details, like Todd had probably given about me. Fine.

"Things were great at first. Then, I don't know when it started, maybe a few months after our first date, but gradually, he began picking at me. Things would bother him and he'd point them out."

Todd frowned when he heard me and one of the cameras turn to catch his reaction.

"Yep. That's the look. The 'I'm displeased with you' look. I don't like your outfit, or the restaurant you picked. You're not punctual. You talk about your mom too much."

I knew I was going to regret this, but I felt reckless and continued on. "You read juvenile books. Your voice is babyish when you talk to kids. You shouldn't sleep in, it's lazy."

Greg looked uncomfortable, but behind him, Director Dave nodded in encouragement.

"Todd doesn't like to hear other people eat. Especially chips. I stopped eating chips around him." I shuddered.

Someone sat down next to me on the bench. I looked over expecting Tyson, but it was Carter. "Tell them about your family, Bethany."

A deep breath escaped and I realized I was very close to tears. That would be the worst. Crying about my ex on TV. I shot Carter a grateful glance and began talking about my mom and how she'd finally met someone after being a widow for fifteen years. How my brother had recently married and my mom walked him down the aisle and then he walked her down the aisle a week later. I talked about losing my dad when I was fourteen and how much I missed him. And I cried. I was glad I cried for my dad on camera and not for Todd. Todd didn't deserve another one of my tears.

I walked off after the interview and Carter followed me. I kept walking until I had no choice but to turn around and acknowledge him. I'm not sure why I didn't want to talk to him. He'd just saved my botched interview, after all, but I was wary of anyone crowding me in at this point.

"What's up?" I asked, glancing around for Holly. Hopefully she was being restrained somewhere and not hiding in the bushes waiting to tackle me to the ground for talking to her man. There was no Holly in sight, but a cameraman came up behind us and ran around to catch our conversation. I'd never get used to the constant cameras.

"I wanted to apologize, for saying anything about Todd. It obviously affected your interview back there." He shrugged and stuck his hands in his pockets. "I guess I feel a bit protective of you."

I wasn't sure whether to be offended or flattered. "Why do you feel protective of me?" Not that I wanted to turn down his protection. On this show I might need it.

"I..." Whatever he meant to say, he must have decided against it. "I like you. That's all."

"You don't even know me." It sounded rude, but there were cameras everywhere and all I kept thinking about was how Tyson thought everyone was acting.

Carter smiled. "I know. But I'd like to get to know you better."

He had the most amazing smile. Even his smile wrinkles were adorable. They betrayed the fact that he probably smiled a lot. He kept his eyes on mine in a way that made me feel like the most important, most beautiful woman in the world. I couldn't help smiling back, but my mouth was a traitor. I didn't want to feel all gooey inside yet. This show was a hot mess and I needed to be in control of myself.

As we walked, he took my arm. Such a gentlemanly and old fashioned gesture. And he had a rock hard bicep, which I pretty much expected. I was tempted to squeeze it, but I resisted. We continued walking slowly around the apartment complex and didn't say another word to each other for ten whole minutes. It felt like we were on the set of *Downton Abbey*, instead of making circles around a shabby apartment complex lawn. Another five minutes went by and the cameraman got bored and wandered away. He had filmed us walking together from every possible angle and we'd given him nothing more to work with.

"How did you do that?" I whispered out of the corner of my mouth. I didn't turn my head toward him, afraid the cameramen would see us talking again and swarm.

"I didn't know if it would work, but I feel more relaxed now. Don't you?"

"Yeah. I do."

"My dad is a 911 operator. He likes to go for walks after work with my mom to relax. They walk around the neighborhood until dinner time."

"911, I bet that's a stressful job."

"Yep. People call in a panic, screaming, and then he turns it over to the police and never knows if everything turned out okay. And he's heard a lot of awful things. When I was a kid he worked nights. I'd try to wait up for him, but end up falling asleep. I remember one time he came into my room after I'd gone to bed. I woke up because he held me and cried." He blushed. "Sorry, I'm talking too much about me."

I wanted to ask more about his family, but sensed he wanted to change the subject.

"Where are you from?" I asked.

"Minot, North Dakota. Born and raised. What about you?"

"Phoenix, Arizona."

He looked at me like I was crazy. "It gets to be 120 degrees there. My aunt lives in Phoenix and she always visits us in summer to get out of the heat."

"I love it. I hate winter. I hate snow." I raised an eyebrow. "I've been to North Dakota in summer. The mosquitoes ate me alive."

Carter wasn't going down without a fight. "But you have scorpions and tarantulas."

"I've been stung by scorpions a few times. It's not that bad. It's like a bee sting. And I've never seen a tarantula outside of a zoo."

"What about tumbleweeds. Are they a myth?"

"Let's just say you could have a successful weed control business in Phoenix. I will concede that point." I was about to come up with another insult for North Dakota, but Greg was franticly waving at us and sent an assistant over to bring us back. Free time was over.

CHAPTER 5

Large umbrellas and lounge chairs had been set up by the pool. They instructed us to start casual conversation with each other. To save time, they had three stations so when we were done with one interaction, we immediately moved to the next station and chatted with another contestant in a round robin of sorts. There was a lot of whining about it until they started handing out margaritas.

I was having a hard time being normal sober, so I drank a lot of lemonade out of tall pretty glasses. They required a drink in your hand at all times, thinking it made us look relaxed and glamourous or something. Well, trailer park glamourous. They still kept reminding us this show was more down-to-earth than any show ever. Sure.

As they led me to the first set of chairs, I recognized the back of Todd's head. I turned and glared at Dave.

"Really?"

Dave smirked at me. "Don't worry, sweetheart. You don't have to be nice to him. In fact, we'd prefer it if you weren't."

How reassuring. I plopped down in the chair opposite Todd and took a long drink of lemonade.

Todd eyed me in a bored way and started chuckling. "Nice interview earlier. You made me sound like a real piece of work."

"Why are you laughing about it?"

Todd smiled at me. "You came off catty. I'm not worried."

"Then why are we talking about it?"

"Ooh, defensive." Todd's eyes gleamed. "I had an interview

about you, too."

"I'm aware of that." I tried to sound uninterested, but Todd could read me well. He waited, looking me up and down, taking in my ugly outfit, as if it was my fault. My jeans sat so high they were creating weird bulges around my midsection. I tried not to think about it.

"How's the job going?" I asked, changing the subject.

"Great. I got a raise. Got a new apartment. It's super nice. I have dinner parties on my balcony. It's that big."

"Congratulations."

Todd seemed pleased I'd brought up his work. "How's your job? You still back up DJ or something?"

Jerk. As a communications major, I'd first thought I wanted to be a radio DJ. My misguided childhood dream. My one and only stint as a DJ lasted about two weeks, before they realized it wasn't just nerves. The station could have fired me, but I got moved to advertising instead. And I was dang good at it.

I glared at Todd. "Job's fine." He didn't need to know that when I got back home I'd have to get back on the air again. I took a deep breath.

Todd leaned forward. "They asked what you were like, you know, while we were dating."

"And what was I like?" Might as well get it over with.

"I said you were sweet, but not smart or assertive enough for me. That you were stuck in a dead-end job and a dead-end relationship, but you were happy with mediocre. That I was ready to move on when you still thought everything was fine."

I had no words. Todd could be nice when he wanted to, but never genuinely nice. It was easy to see in hindsight. He'd hid his true self pretty well while we were dating, but I'd caught glimpses of it with slow waiters or co-workers on the phone. And now he'd turned it in full force, jabbing me as best he could. He was right about one thing, I didn't see our relationship as a dead-end until it was actually, well, dead.

"Oh, and that pretty boy you were hanging on earlier? If the vein popping out of his head was any indication, he didn't like what I had to say in my interview." Todd stood up and smiled down at me. "He can't wait to be your knight-in-shining-armor. You're welcome."

You're welcome? I stifled a scream and shook out my shoulders, trying to relax. This was what this show wants, I reminded myself. Drama. Lots and lots of drama.

They brought Marco over, still in his silky boxer shorts, damp from the pool. He sipped his drink and studied me. Finally he said, "Bethany, you are a beautiful woman."

I blushed and tried to think of a good response, but Marco saved me by launching into a story about himself. Every time there was a lull in the conversation he'd repeat in that sexy accent of his, "Bethany, you are a beautiful woman." I had to admit, I liked hearing him say it. Especially after the way Todd had looked at me.

"Why did you try out for a show like this?" I asked.

"I like women," he responded, as if that was all the explanation necessary.

My third chat was with Holly. She sized me up with a look of pure hatred and loathing and some of the tension in my neck returned. I imagined her red hair bursting into flames. Greg suggested a few prompts to get us started, but Holly sat there with her arms folded and stared at me. So maybe I wasn't paranoid for thinking she might hide in the bushes and jump me.

Finally, she leaned forward and asked, "What were you and Carter talking about all that time over there?"

"Um, where we're from and stuff like that."

"I've known Carter since kindergarten." *So back off,* her tone seemed to say.

After a few more minutes of silent treatment I decided to have a one-sided conversation. I started talking about my favorite shampoo. I talked about the way it smelled, how it made my hair more manageable and how once I'd driven across town to get it because my salon had run out. I looked over at Greg and he nodded, as if to say, "Good enough."

They let me up for a bathroom break, but I stopped to eavesdrop on Max and Michelle before leaving. Max was saying, "No one ever picks me for anything. I'm like the oatmeal raisin cookie on the dessert tray. This was all about getting Anna here, obviously. I mean, would you pick me for a show like this?" I caught Michelle's eye and she gave me an exasperated smile.

***

When I got back they sat me down with Patrick, Michelle's ex. He was lanky, all arms and legs, but handsome in his own way and extremely nervous about all the cameras, even more than me. I was curious about him, since Michelle had said they broke up in college over a practical joke. It would be rude to ask Patrick about it, considering we'd barely met, so instead I wondered about it while going through the usual boring questions like where he was from and what he did for a living.

I should have been paying attention, but I was already tired of interviews and cameras and talking about myself. I know I missed something because Patrick was staring at me for a reaction and the pause became really awkward, and then I remembered he'd made a joke. I laughed belatedly, mumbling something about the heat, even though we were under umbrellas and eighty degrees was perfect for a desert rat like me.

Dave finally let us go. I ran upstairs and collapsed on my twin bed after peeling away the scratchy comforter like Michelle had earlier. I meant to wait for Michelle so I could ask her about Patrick, but that was my last thought before waking up to the sound of arguing.

"I haven't seen you in six years and then you show up here! I came on this show for love. I know that makes me just another idiot, but seeing you makes me realize how stupid this was. And I thought internet dating was for suckers."

"Shh, Patrick. Calm down. They'll hear you and want to film us. I can't believe no one followed you."

Michelle paced in and out of my view, glancing around as if she suspected hidden cameras. I didn't know what to do. I wanted to escape without being a total eavesdropper, but I'd listened long enough, it was going to be awkward no matter what. The best thing to do at this point was stay in bed. I closed my eyes and pretended not to enjoy the soap opera for my ears.

"Every time I look at you I remember how beautiful and cruel you were. You ruined my life you know."

"Don't be so dramatic. You're a successful accountant."

So that's what he did for a living. I'd have to remember from now on. Man, Michelle did sound cruel.

I heard shuffling, then Michelle murmuring 'don't' and then kissing, and then Patrick said something I couldn't determine, but it sounded like begging and then a door slamming and then Michelle crying. Oh snap. The crying was getting closer. What to do? I kicked out of the sheets and ran into the bathroom, closing the door as quietly as I could.

Panicking, I turned on the shower and twirled around, looking for a place to sit. Strangely, our toilet had no lid and I wasn't about to plop down on the toilet seat for a chair. It didn't look like the sink would hold my weight if I tried to jump up and sit on it. That would be awesome to explain. Just doing some remodeling in here!

There were two bath towels on a rod above the toilet, but the towels looked small and I didn't know where they'd been and I wanted my towel from my bag if I actually was going to shower. And I needed an elastic to put my hair up because I wasn't about to wash it right now and I didn't have my shampoo. Or soap. Or a razor. This was stupid. I turned off the shower water and walked out of the bathroom.

Michelle was lying on her bed staring at the ceiling. "Are you done with your pretend shower already?"

I gaped at her. "How did you know?"

"I saw you run for the bathroom. I like you, but if it's all the same to you, I don't feel like talking about this with someone I met today."

"It's okay. I won't say anything. And I won't ask you about it." I turned to go. "Do you know what we're supposed to be doing right now?"

"Dave is filming the guys asking us out on individual dates. I already got asked out by Max. He gave me a daisy Greg handed him two seconds before we filmed it. It was really romantic."

I laughed. "Sounds fun. I guess I'll head down there then." Michelle clearly needed some alone time.

About five steps down the stairs, an assistant stopped me and told me I'd need a wardrobe change. Director Dave was probably trying to make it look like a different day. Cheapo. Now that I thought about it, Michelle had been wearing jean overalls over a neon green tie-dye T-shirt during her argument with Patrick. Not sure how I missed that.

I headed back upstairs and went into to the closet to have a look. Everything was ugly, but there were endless choices of ugly.

"Forgot to mention the wardrobe change," Michelle said, still staring at the ceiling. "I miss my phone. A good game of Angry Birds would really cheer me up right now."

I tried on a pair of khaki cargo pants and gagged. They made me look three feet wide. I pulled them off and tried on some hot pink leggings that felt like they were made of plastic. Maybe if I had something long to put over them. I found a grey sweater dress and a wide silver belt with a gaudy buckle and went with it. Judging by Michelle's clothing choices, we were all giving up on normal.

CHAPTER 6

Downstairs, I found Greg and he paired me up with Weston, the only guy without a date yet. "Who's Weston?" I whispered to Tyson, who was lounging nearby eating Oreos. I suddenly craved their chocolatey goodness. I grabbed one before realizing it would be all over my teeth if I ate it, so I put it back.

"You're not dieting are you?" Tyson asked, scolding me. "Your figure is perfect, as is mine."

Then I noticed his outfit. "What are you wearing?" He was shirtless, of course, but that was normal compared to his tiny cutoffs and laceless Keds. I wanted to grab something to drape over his thighs.

Greg came over and took my arm. "Bethany, we need you over here with Weston."

I'd never gotten an answer from Tyson about who Weston was. Dang Tyson and dang Oreos. Completely distracting. I tried to connect the dots as they pinned a microphone to me and the makeup artist buffed my complexion. Tyson was Gretchen's ex. Todd was mine. Marco was Jada's. Eddie was Sylvie's ex. Michelle and Patrick, Holly and Carter. Who did Weston belong to? I'd forgotten someone.

Greg handed Weston a pink carnation and demonstrated how he should casually walk over, sit across from me and hand me the flower.

I studied Weston while they talked. He was very handsome, but short. At 5'6 we were eye to eye. His biceps were bulging out of his

32

shirt sleeves. Clearly he liked to lift weights.

They filmed him walking up to me four times. I had to pretend not to see him until he sat down in the chair across from me, and then I had to act surprised and pleased. It was harder than I thought.

"Hi Bethany. I've been meaning to talk to you. I was hoping we could spend some time together." He handed me the flower like it was a spontaneous gesture and not planned out. "Will you be my first date?"

"Yes, Weston. I'd love to."

And that was that. They rushed me off to have an on-camera heart-to-heart with Michelle, and I still knew absolutely nothing about Weston.

I headed back to our apartment with an entourage of cameramen, director, host, various executives and assistants. We found Michelle cross-legged on her bed, getting her makeup done. She was in plaid pajamas and as soon as I'd gotten in pajama pants and a T-shirt they pulled the curtains and dimmed the lights. It couldn't have been later than 4:00 p.m. Was nothing about this show ever going to be real? Well the cookies were going to be real. I spotted another Oreo package in the hands of an assistant and swiped them.

While the director and camera crew were moving things around, I took the opportunity to ask Michelle about Weston. She grinned. "You missed a lot while you were asleep. Max is Anna's ex, but he was a rebound after Weston, the love of her life. Do you remember her blubbering about him this morning? How she broke off their engagement? Greg claims Weston stormed in here, demanding another chance with her. That he changed his mind and wanted on the show after all. He's probably an actor they found. Poor Max. Not exciting enough for a show like this. He'll probably get voted off first."

"But what about *Seven Brides for Seven Brothers*?" I asked, biting into an Oreo.

Michelle stared back at me as if I'd grown a third arm. "What?"

I blushed. "I figured with seven guys and seven girls they had a theme going."

Michelle laughed at me. "Hand me a cookie."

After we'd mowed through half the package, we ran and brushed our teeth and then sat on the beds.

They had plenty of guidance as far as what they wanted us to say. I listened to Michelle gush about how excited she was for her date with Max and then I took my turn and gushed about Weston. I even claimed I might try to steal him from Anna if he turned out to be 'The One.' The whole thing was utter nonsense and took incredibly long. They made us do personal interviews afterwards, where we answered question after question, knowing most of it would never get used.

After the crew left, Michelle opened the curtains and peeked out to make sure they were gone. She quickly changed back into the outfit she came in, minus the nametag, and gave me a sneaky smile. "If anyone asks, I went to find the ice machine." And then she was gone. Most likely, she was off to find Patrick while the crew was filming Gretchen and Sylvie's heart-to-heart. Good for her.

I thought about polishing off the package of Oreos and painting my toenails. But that's what the old me would do, the introverted me who had been pining over Todd. Not so much pining over him, I decided. Pining over the loss of me. The fun me. And I wanted her back.

There was no point in sitting in this shabby apartment by myself, even if going outside meant more cameras. I put away the Oreo package, put on some lip gloss and slipped my shoes back on. As I was heading for the door I heard a soft knock. I cracked the door and saw Weston, of all people.

"Hey." I looked behind him for cameras but there weren't any.

"We need a fourth for poker? You in?"

I shrugged. "Sure. Where are you playing?"

"Meet us in apartment seven in five minutes. And bring snacks if you have any. I don't know what they expect us to do for dinner, but we're all starving."

I wondered who else was playing and what money they were using. I had maybe ten dollars in cash. A search of the kitchenette cupboards revealed a package of microwave popcorn and a box of granola bars. Hopefully the staff of the reality show had put them there and they hadn't been sitting for years, left by some former tenant. I grabbed them and the leftover Oreos and headed over to apartment seven.

"Hey, you made it!" Tyson greeted me at the door, but my eyes were drawn to Carter, sitting on the couch in the background. My heart sped up at the sight of him. I knew it was ridiculous. Good-looking guys blinded you from seeing who they really were. Todd had taught me that. And Carter was way better looking than Todd. He made Todd look like a lawn gnome.

I sat down at the kitchen table and pulled out my cash: a five, three ones and two quarters.

Tyson laughed. "Put it away, Bethany. We're too poor to play for money. That's why we're all on this show."

"Speak for yourself," Weston called from the bedroom. "I'm a lawyer."

"So your script says," Tyson shot back. "There aren't any cameras in here. Admit you're a struggling actor."

Weston came out and leaned on the door jamb. "I'm not an actor. I was engaged to Anna and I am a lawyer. The show contacted me months ago to come on here with Anna. I told them no and promised not to say anything to her about it. But then when they came back and said she was going to be on the show with an ex anyway, I called in a few favors at the firm and freed up my schedule."

Carter, Tyson and I studied him, trying to decide if he was lying.

"And you're trying to win her back?" I asked.

"Well…" Weston shrugged. "That's the show's version. I'm just trying to keep her from hooking up with some wannabe reality star. Like him." He pointed at Tyson.

"Whatever, man. If I was a better poker player I'd test out your story and win some of that lawyer money for myself. But I rarely win so we're playing with candy."

Tyson pulled a bag of conversation hearts out of a cupboard and tossed them on the table.

Weston poked at them and frowned. "This package is old. How many Valentines ago are these from?"

"Relax, prima donna. We're not eating them, we're gambling." Tyson ripped open the bag and picked one up. GET REAL. "This one's for you." He tossed it to Weston and then divvied out the rest while Carter shuffled the cards.

Carter had been awfully quiet while the two other guys bickered. But he caught me watching him and smiled. "I'm glad you're here. I'm stuck with these two as roommates, at least until one of them gets voted off."

"Like I'm leaving anytime soon," Tyson scoffed. "As soon as someone tips off Anna that Romeo here isn't interested in her anymore, no one is going to vote for him."

"And you're their top pick?" Weston responded.

I was starting to question my eagerness to leave my apartment. I liked Tyson and Weston better when they weren't acting like competing alpha males in a walrus herd. I'd seen a National Geographic special on it once. I stifled a giggle thinking of the two of them bellowing at each other and baring their tusks.

Carter stealthily slid over a heart that said YOU'RE TOPS. I smiled and sent him one back that said TOO SWEET. Tyson noticed us and slid one over for me. SO FINE. I wasn't sure if he was referring to me or himself. I found DIVA in my pile and handed it over to Tyson and nodded toward Weston. Tyson slid it over to him and naturally it set Weston off. He flicked it off the table.

"Are we going to play poker or not? You guys are like children."

Tyson and I busted out laughing, but we quieted when there was a sharp rapping at the door. We all looked over with dread, knowing the cameras had found us.

"Carter, are you in there?" Holly called through the door. Carter's shoulders slumped and he got up to answer it. Holly pushed her way in as soon as the door cracked open, followed by two cameramen, Greg, and Director Dave.

Greg gave us his best 'concerned father' look. "Dave would like me to explain that from now on, you should ask for a cameraman to follow you before socializing with other contestants."

Holly stood next to him, nodding in agreement. "Carter, you should have invited me. Especially with *her* in here."

I resisted the obvious invitation into a girl fight and scooted over so Holly could squeeze in a chair next to him. Carter dealt the cards and we got down to a serious game of poker. Well, as serious as you can get playing with leftover Valentines candy.

Crazy Holly surprisingly had a great poker face and was an excellent bluffer. She won the first hand with only a pair of kings and the next one with an ace high. I assumed Tyson would be an aggressive better, but he folded to Holly's ace with a pair of jacks.

We took a break for pizza the show brought from a nearby restaurant. I noticed Holly had gradually scooted closer to Carter over the course of the game until she was practically in his lap. She was playing with her big pile of conversation hearts and showed one to Carter. It said CRAZY 4 U. They laughed and ducked their heads. I wondered what their private joke meant, but felt weird for eavesdropping and stared down at my own small pile of hearts. I was one of those mediocre poker players who bet conservatively enough to never win or lose. I realized I had applied that strategy to many things in my life, including my career and my love life. And it wasn't just Todd getting into my head. Coming on this show had been my desperate attempt to be a risk taker.

"Why the frown?" Tyson asked.

"Too much introspection," I answered. "It's a habit of mine."

"Don't over think this," Tyson whispered. "Bethany, this is an acting gig. And the sooner you treat it that way the easier it will be."

"But I'm not an actor."

"Not yet. But you'll get used to the cameras, and when you do, you'll know how fake all this is."

Our faces were very close and a cameraman was trained right on us. I smiled and touched Tyson's cheek. "I think you're right," I said, loud enough for the cameras to pick up. "I'm very glad I met you."

"Right back at yah, babe." Tyson slid his arm around my shoulder and gave it a squeeze.

I felt Carter's eyes on me and refused to look at him. Like he had any reason to care with Holly all over him. Tyson was right. If I was going to start a relationship on this show, it shouldn't be complicated by real feelings. The thought was disappointing, but a foregone conclusion after a day swarmed by cameras.

After the game wrapped up, Tyson walked me to my door and gave me a really long hug, his face pressed against my hair.

"Are you sniffing my hair?" I asked, giggling.

"It smells good."

"I know."

Tyson laughed. "You're starting to sound like me."

I pressed my cheek against his and let him hold me a little longer. Carter's face popped into my mind and I tried unsuccessfully to push him out. Maybe it was heartless to hold someone and wish it was someone else, but I didn't think Tyson would mind. And who knew, maybe he was thinking of someone, too.

CHAPTER 7

Greg, Dave and the crew knocked on the door just as Michelle and I were getting desperate enough to consider eating microwave popcorn for breakfast. Thankfully, the crew stocked our pantry and fridge while assistants fixed our hair and makeup.

"We want to film your morning routine, while you talk about your activities last night," Greg explained.

Out of the corner of my eye I saw Michelle stiffen. With that terrible poker face it was a good thing she missed out on our game.

"Great!" I said, trying to deflect attention away from Michelle. "I want to talk about Tyson. Does that work for you?" Michelle nodded vigorously and started peppering me with questions about Tyson over our bowls of cereal. About a minute into it I realized I probably should be careful about talking with my mouth full and tried to be more ladylike as I ate. It would have been easier if I wasn't so hungry.

"Okay, Michelle. It's your turn. We need you to add more to the conversation," Greg said. "Tell us something juicy."

Oh no. Deer-in-the-headlights was back. "Didn't you go talk to Anna about Weston?" I prompted.

"Oh, yes." Michelle said. "She's torn between Weston and Max. And that was hard for me to hear because I'm looking forward to my date with Max tonight."

We continued on with my made-up story until Director Dave felt we'd given him enough. He'd insisted we keep eating as we talked and I was sorry I'd been so eager to wolf down my first two bowls of cereal. Even I have my limits on Cinnamon Toast Crunch.

Greg gave us instructions on when and where to meet for our dates that night and what to wear. A cameraman stayed behind to film Michelle washing the dishes and then we were instructed to come down to the pool at our leisure for more 'casual interactions.'

Thankfully, the tacky clothes did not extend to swimsuits. They had a whole row of brand-new ones in the closet. However, they did not believe in one pieces. Every single swimsuit was a teeny-tiny bikini that barely met the requirement of covering up my lady parts. I sighed. Part and parcel to being on TV. After choosing one, I added a pair of running shorts and a towel over my shoulders.

Most of the contestants were already at the pool when I got there. A cameraman was filming one of the guys doing laps. In the tiny pool, a lap consisted of about four swimming strokes, but the guy was doing his best to get some exercise. When he surfaced I recognized Patrick. He grinned at me, but his eyes glanced upstairs. I gave a small nod to indicate that yes, Michelle was still up there and then sat down on a lounge chair next to Jada. I opened my book and had finally settled into the storyline enough to forget where I was, when Todd and Sylvie came downstairs together giggling and grabbing at each other.

Oh gag. They sat down across the pool from me and started making out. A cameraman followed behind them the whole time, like a devoted peeping tom. Which was an unfair judgment considering I couldn't stop staring either.

"Todd's your ex, right?" Jada asked.

I nodded. "It's like a train wreck. I can't look away."

"Bad breakup?"

"He got a job promotion that required him to move to another state. But we still talked every night and I planned a trip to visit him. The day before I left, I tried calling and texting him, but he didn't respond. When I got to his new apartment he didn't answer the door. I thought maybe I'd gotten the address wrong. He finally called me when I was sitting alone in my hotel room that night. He said he'd met someone else so he didn't need a long distance relationship anymore." I couldn't believe I'd admitted that to Jada.

"For real? He did that to you?" Jada sat up and pulled off her sunglasses. "A lousy cheater like that doesn't deserve the air he's breathing."

"He didn't see it as cheating. He said I should have known. Didn't even apologize."

"Does Sylvie know this?"

I shook my head. "I didn't know the two were hitting it off until this morning."

"Well we should do something. That piece of garbage shouldn't be strutting around here like…"

"Like a rooster in a hen house?"

"Okay, we'll go with your reference. Anyway, he deserves some payback."

The gleam in her eye was scaring me and I knew I needed to talk her down fast.

"Jada, relax. He's not worth it. Remember, you're on camera."

She was already standing up. "Oh, I'm aware of the cameras. I got this, honey."

I watched her take her time sauntering over to where Todd and Sylvie were canoodling. She even stopped to ask Greg a question. But eventually she made her way to their lounge chairs. Jada leaned over and whispered something to Sylvie and then glanced at Todd.

"Hey buddy, eyes up here," she said, loudly.

Todd put his hands up in surrender and blushed. I couldn't hear what he said, but Sylvie frowned and crossed her arms. Clever Jada. She made sure to catch Todd appreciating her assets, thanks to the tiny swimwear provided. And by calling him out on it in front of Sylvie, she had no choice but to take offense. Now Todd was stalking off in one direction and Sylvie in the other. Both were followed by cameras. Priceless.

Jada gave me a little wave as she bounced over to Marco who was coming downstairs. I went back to my book until I became too drowsy to continue.

I woke up to a shadow over me with a familiar scent. Though I couldn't quite place it, it made me feel unsettled. I blinked and saw Todd staring down at me. A cameraman was behind him, and I sensed the one behind me. A camera ambush. I was pretty sure I'd have to get used to that.

"You're blocking my sun," I said as casually as possible.

"I know you put Jada up to that little stunt." Todd glared at me and then had the nerve to move my legs so he could sit on my patio chair.

"Obviously you don't know Jada, because she does whatever she wants. I didn't tell her to do anything."

"Whatever. You told her a bunch of lies about me then. Sylvie won't even talk to me."

"You've known Sylvie for like five minutes. I think you'll be okay."

"Being jealous does not give you the right to belittle me."

I wanted to be calm. I needed to be calm. But Todd was a master at pushing buttons, even fake ones. "I'm not jealous."

Todd grinned. "Are you sure? Do you need attention? Is that it?" He tucked a lock of my hair behind my ear, like he used to do when we were together, only now it made me sick to my stomach. And was he leaning in?

"Oh, don't flatter yourself." I pushed him away and sat up so fast my book tumbled off of my chest. "I am over you, Todd. OVER you." Oh my gosh, I was sounding like Holly. Director Dave even gave me a thumbs up. I stood up and walked off, realizing I was shaking. I was not cut out for this. Not with Todd here. But maybe Jada's interference was enough to get him eliminated tomorrow night. I could only hope.

***

I was almost to my room when I realized Patrick and Michelle were probably in there and a cameraman was still following me. Knowing there was a little alcove with a vending machine at the end of the corridor, I passed my apartment and headed there. I didn't have any money on me (bikinis generally don't have pockets) but I could pretend to browse. I was so intent on my plan, I almost smacked into Carter coming around the corner from the vending machine. He held up his soda protectively.

"Okay, you caught me. I admit, I'm addicted to Dr. Pepper."

"Your secret's safe with me, and the rest of America," I said, gesturing to the camera. We stood there grinning at each other and I didn't know why I couldn't move around him and continue on. We'd exchanged pleasantries. Wasn't this the part where he said, 'Well, good to see you,' and continued on his way?

"What's your plan this morning?" he asked.

I shrugged. "Nothing I guess. What about you?"

"No idea. I'm a little lost without a daily schedule."

"A daily schedule?"

He turned a little red. "Yeah, I like lists. I like to have plans, even for a day off. You know, all my errands, laundry, washing pots and pans because I tend to let them pile up, mail to sort, sit-up goals, not that you need to know I do sit-ups. I…I like to track my progress."

He reminded me of the way I talk when I'm nervous. Was I making him nervous?

"I'm going to stop talking now."

"No, no," I said, trying to keep from laughing. "You're adorable." Oh man, now I was blushing. "I mean, it's adorable that you make lists and stuff." Now we both sounded like idiots. The cameraman was probably rolling his eyes.

"Would you like to have a do nothing day with me?" Carter blurted out.

"Of course." I wanted to pinch myself. I shouldn't sound so eager. It was embarrassing. And could he cover up his chest now? I think I was checking him out more than he was checking me out. Dang all this swimwear. "I'm going to go change into something…something else first."

"Oh, me too."

I felt both relieved and disappointed. "Great, I'll meet you downstairs in ten minutes."

As I walked back to my apartment, I tried to think of a way to lose the cameraman following behind. "Hey," I said turning to face him. "I'm going to change out of my swimsuit. I don't think it needs to be filmed."

"Just doing my job," the cameraman responded before stalking off. Perv.

When I walked in, Michelle was sitting next to Patrick on the couch holding an icepack to the back his head.

"Oh, it's you," Michelle said with obvious relief.

"What the heck happened?"

"Patrick snuck in here. I whacked him with a lamp before I realized it was him."

The ugly lamp Michelle had threatened to throw yesterday lay broken on the floor.

"Yikes. Does he need to go to the hospital?"

Patrick shook his head, then winced. "I'm fine. It's only a goose egg."

"I'm so sorry, baby," Michelle said, stroking his hair. "I figured someone on the staff was a creeper or something."

"You did the right thing," Patrick answered. He looked into her eyes and they were so focused on each other it was as if I'd never come in. I fled to the bedroom to change before things got any mushier. You'd think I would have considered all the uncomfortable public displays of affection I'd be stepping into when I came on a dating show.

I could have stared at the closet of despair for hours if I didn't have Carter waiting for me downstairs or the couple in the other room waiting for me to leave. I finally put on a V-neck shirt with big, purple, gaudy flowers all over it and purple gaucho pants. I'd figured all the gaucho pants in the world had been destroyed long ago, but I guess they'd been tucked away by demented TV producers. They had them in every color.

***

Carter tried not to stare at my outfit. He really did his best, but the purple, loud pants looked even worse reflected in his eyes.

"That bad, huh?"

"I don't know what you're talking about." Carter looked back at me with wide-eyed innocence. He had on a yellow linen shirt with large white polka dots and white jean shorts frayed on the end. Of course, he looked great in anything. If this thing ever aired, he'd probably start a trend.

We walked over to one of the few trees in the courtyard and sat in the shade.

"You ready to bore the camera man to death until he leaves?" Carter whispered.

"Totally."

He stretched out on the grass, tucking one arm behind him like a pillow, and slinging his other arm over his eyes. I studied the ends of my hair, checking for split ends.

After five minutes of silence, the cameraman got irritated. "I know what you two are doing. And it's not going to work."

Carter didn't even flinch so I pretended not to hear and stretched out to catch another nap myself. I made sure to keep enough space between my body and Carter's so there wasn't even the possibility one of us might roll over and spoon the other.

Although I liked the thought of spooning Carter. I let that scene play out in my mind while we waited for the cameraman to go away.

"Give me a few minutes of cheesy camera-loving action and then I'll leave you two alone," the cameraman begged after another ten minutes.

"We're listening," Carter answered, his arm still resting across his face.

"Dave said he wants a love triangle between you two and Tyson. Give me some dialogue, something where you confront her about her feelings for Tyson, and then either get mad at each other or fall into each other's arms. Just make it interesting. And then I'll leave you two duds alone and you can nap 'til date night."

Carter sat up and brushed the grass off. "Sounds good to me. Bethany?"

I nodded, suddenly recalling what my boss said about getting noticed. If that's what Dave wanted, then that's what we'd do. I even had an idea of where to start.

"Tyson warned me about you," I put on my most serious face. I hoped it was serious. I felt like a goof.

"What for? You have nothing to fear from me." Carter took my hand and rubbed his thumb across my palm, back and forth. I blushed, unnerved by how such a small thing could make my heart race.

"Tyson told me to stay away from you. That you would only break my heart."

Carter smiled and leaned in. "That's because he wants you for himself."

His hand was caressing up my arm now, and as he reached the sleeve of my hideous flowered shirt a bubble of laughter built up inside of me, threatening to burst. I forced myself back to serious. "Then I have to decide what I want. You or Tyson. But I'll need some time."

"Let me help you decide."

Carter pulled me into him, trying to be passionate about it, but I sensed he was on the razor's edge of starting to laugh, too. He licked his lips a second before dipping in to kiss me. At the last second I panicked and dodged.

"I can't do that to Tyson," I murmured, staring at the ground. I felt terrible for embarrassing Carter, but I didn't want our first kiss to be a big fake smooch for the cameras. And we barely knew each other. It seemed a bit soon to be pushing the romance. I glanced back at Carter and he had his arms folded, looking amused.

"You're not mad at me?" I asked.

"No. If you're going to kiss me I want you to want it."

"I want to, just not right now."

We glanced at the cameraman and he sighed. "All right, good enough." He got up and left us sitting under the tree.

I almost wished he stayed because you could cut the awkwardness with a knife.

"I'm sorry." I blushed. "I haven't dodged a kiss since a particularly handsy blind date I had a few years ago. Not that I was comparing you to that. Sorry."

"It's not your fault." Carter raked his hands through his hair. "I hate this part of it, the fake storylines and the lack of privacy. I keep asking myself why I'm doing this."

"Why are you doing this?"

Carter stared at me. "If I tell you the truth you can't judge me 'til you hear me out."

I folded my arms. "Okay."

"My little sister needs the exposure for her music career. She has a YouTube channel and we sell cover versions of popular songs. I play the piano, she plays violin, and we both sing. It's her dream. But also...we need the money. She has leukemia. Had I should say. It's in remission. But my family still owes a lot in medical bills. She made me promise not to tell the show and let them turn her into a charity case. But she was hoping if I was able to mention it, people would look us up and buy music."

My first instinct was to pull out my phone and google him. But of course I didn't have my phone. "So she won't ask for charity but she's willing to market you off as man meat?"

He shrugged. "She's a teenage girl. And she's also suffering under the delusion that I'm going to find the love of my life here."

I laughed, but his words stung a little. Was no one here for love? I thought about what Tyson said, that the sooner I accepted this was an acting job the better off I would be. Even Carter had ulterior motives. Man was I gullible. Me and every Reality TV junkie in America.

"I thought you were a junior high choir teacher," I said.

"Guilty."

"That's awesome."

"Sure, until you see the size of my paycheck. It was this or mow lawns for extra money this summer. I don't go back to teaching until September."

"So why music? And why junior high?"

Carter laughed. "I know I'm not about to make it big in the music business. That's my sister's dream. But I love to sing and I love to play music. If you can't do... you teach."

"Did you know they have a piano in the conference room?"

"They do?"

"I saw it when they filmed us opening our packets."

"They wouldn't let us near the conference room. That was for the 'female contestants only.' When I got here, they immediately escorted me upstairs to one of the apartments. We were all squished in together, all seven of us guys thigh to thigh on two couches. I was starting to wonder if I'd signed up for a whole new kind of dating show."

I laughed. "Don't suggest it to Dave, he'd probably do it. 'Surprise, you're gay!'" I instinctively glanced behind me for a camera.

"Relax, Bethany. You don't have to watch everything you say with me. I want to get to know the real you."

I wanted to ask why, but it seemed like I was always trying to question his motives. "So why don't you give me piano lessons? That way you could get your music mentioned."

"You'd do that for me?"

"Of course. I've always wanted to learn piano, and we have nothing but time around here."

"Okay, let's go see this piano."

We walked over to the conference room, but the door was locked. Even if we could get in on our own, Dave would want to recreate us finding it. Great, more acting.

Carter sighed. "We need to present this to Dave so he'll want to devote some camera time to it. Any ideas?"

"I'll tell him I have a thing for musicians. I think he'll buy it."

Dave and Greg were busy filming an intense breakup/makeup make-out scene between Jada and Marco and couldn't be bothered with us. But they had lunch set up so Carter and I sat down under an umbrella and ate.

I couldn't help stealing glances at Carter while he was helping himself to seconds. What was going on with him and Holly? Why did he keep saying he wanted to get to know me? He'd basically said he was only here for his sister.

And as I was having these thoughts Holly walked up and dragged him off. Carter glanced back at me apologetically, but didn't try to stop her.

Was this what I would have to put up with on a show like this? I tried to calm myself down. *Silly Bethany, so possessive after one day, and over a guy who's not even interested.* He didn't mind that I chickened out of kissing him because he didn't care either way. I finished my sandwich, forcing Carter out of my mind.

CHAPTER 8

After lunch, they ordered me upstairs to film more heart-to-heart chats, which was a nice way of saying they wanted on-camera gossip to craft into their implausible storylines. I wasn't concerned about it until I realized they were filming me knocking on Sylvie's door. I knew it was going to be awkward, but the look Sylvie gave me only reaffirmed how little either of us wanted to see each other.

Greg set the tone with this nice little suggestion. "Bethany, why don't you give Sylvie some insight into your ex, Todd. And then Sylvie can share about her budding relationship with him. It will be fun!" We both glared at him.

"Do we have to?" Sylvie whined. "This show is supposed to be about finding romance and you guys are killing it." Her voice had started wavering and I felt sorry for her. Sorry they were ruining things for her, but mostly sorry she wanted to find romance with Todd. Greg pretended he hadn't heard her and motioned for me to start.

"So Sylvie, I wanted to talk to you about Todd."

"What about him?" she responded, arms folded defensively.

"I… I think…" Forget it. If she wanted to date Todd, what was the harm? It's not like she was marrying him. "I think he likes you."

"Really? What makes you say that?"

"He told me. He was very upset when Jada tricked him earlier and you ran off." I left out the part where he tried to make a move on me, whether he meant it as joke or not.

Sylvie beamed. "Yeah, he came and apologized. He told me he couldn't stop thinking about me."

"How great for you."

"So you two are still friends then? Even though he's your ex?" Sylvie's eyes shined with hope.

"We still talk." *Because we're on a show together.*

"That's good. What about you? Who do you have your eye on?" She leaned over like we were two pre-teen girls gossiping at a sleepover.

My mind immediately flitted to Carter, but I felt protective of my feelings for him and embarrassed that I had any. "Oh, I like Tyson. He's so genuine and funny."

Sylvie smiled, but it was almost like a grimace. "Tyson? Really? Gretchen told me he's such a child."

I wanted to make a snide remark about where Gretchen and Eddie had been all day but it would have been a low blow to mention Sylvie's ex to her. "Tyson is fun to be around. I'm attracted to guys with a sense of humor."

Sylvie sniffed. "Well, I figured you'd want to know a little about him before you jump into a relationship."

Dave and Greg were watching me intently and Dave nodded slowly, as if to say, 'Now! Zing her now! You have all this dirt on Todd.' I forced myself to look away from them and back into Sylvie's eyes.

"Is there anything you want to know about Todd then?" I would leave it up to her. If Dave wanted to humiliate her he could do it in editing.

Sylvie sat back and fiddled with a hole in her stonewashed jeans. "Did he treat you well?"

"No. Not really."

"Oh." Her face dropped and she studied me for a minute, as if trying to figure out if I'd said it as a joke. "But he's always been super nice to me. Are you sure you're not picturing it that way now, you know, because he dumped you?"

This was so pointless. "Yep, he was a perfect gentleman, as long as I didn't do anything that upset him or disappointed him. Good luck with that."

I stood up and walked off before Sylvie had a chance to respond, giving her a little wave on my way out.

Michelle was digging through the closet when I got back to our apartment. I knew she was in there because I could hear her curses all the way from the front door. Clothes were strewn all over the bed and floor.

"I'm running out of options." She whipped through the rack again, dismissing every possible outfit. "I can't decide what to wear for our date tonight. Not that I care what Max thinks, but I know this date is not going to get edited out. Millions of people are going to see me in these sorry excuses for fashion."

I flipped through her side of the closet and pulled out a powder blue velour jogging suit. "I dare you to wear this."

Michelle considered. "I've tried that on before. It's super ugly, but it does make my butt look good."

"Have they said what we're doing on this date?" I asked. "Do you think we'll leave the apartment complex?" It was only day two and I was already feeling cagey.

"That would be nice. But no, we're supposed to make dinner together and play games or something lame."

"Great, board games. I already know Weston is a sore loser. He was not much fun at poker last night." I pulled out a polyester button-down and tried it on. It managed to make me look flat-chested and fat at the same time. I put it back and tried on a few more tops before I was satisfied.

After we dressed and finished putting on makeup, we sat and watched TV until it was time for our dates. We laughed at reruns of Project Runway, noting that even some of our recent outfits weren't as bad as the stuff those contestants came up with.

Michelle got a gleam in her eye. "If only we had a sewing machine. We could transform some of that garbage in the closet."

"I don't think Dave would let us."

Michelle sighed. "Probably not."

***

The film crew came at five, leading us down to the apartment Max shared with Eddie. Eddie was off in some holding area. They'd explained earlier that our group dates were filmed in shifts, so our date would probably be done in a few hours and the rest of our night would be free. Or so I hoped. Being put in a holding area sounded a lot like jail.

Max welcomed us in, looking nervous as usual, and we all

congregated around the kitchen counter where we'd be making fajitas. Weston came a minute later and gave me a nice hug, but then Dave sent an assistant over to make us redo it. They hadn't been able to film it from the right angle the first time. Weston threw a mini-tantrum, as if having to hug me a second time was too much for him.

It was a relief to get back to the business of chopping vegetables and adding them to the pan. This was familiar to me and kept me from having to think of the right things to say. We cooked in quiet cooperation for a few minutes, but Dave was not happy with our lack of conversation. The assistants brought out new vegetables for us to chop while we regurgitated some of the suggested talking points Greg and Dave came up with.

Greg put a bowl of conversation starters in the middle of the table and told us to each choose one during dinner.

I opened mine up with some reluctance. *What are you afraid of?*

My mind immediately went to work. Death, clowns, getting lost somewhere scary, crowded buses, salmonella poisoning, Chihuahua dogs. Oh man, I really didn't want anyone to know about that last one. When I read my prompt aloud, I mentioned only my fear of crowded buses. I knew everyone would start chiming in about claustrophobia and sure enough, Max shuddered and told us a story about being in a crowded subway car that was delayed for three hours. It was a bad enough tale that I didn't want to eat my fajitas for a few minutes.

"Please tell me someone has a happy one," Michelle begged.

"All right, here's mine," Weston said. "Do you use pickup lines?" He grinned. "Of course."

Max turned to him with some interest. "I never use pickup lines. I tried it once and it was disastrous."

Weston was happy to explain. "You have to have confidence, man. Like you know it's going to work."

"So what pickup line do you use?" Michelle asked. "Cause the last guy that tried one on me got laughed out of the place by me and my friends."

"Oh no. I never approach a woman surrounded by her friends. She's gotta be on her own."

Max was listening intently. "And what do you say?"

Weston paused for effect. "One I've had pretty good success with is, 'Can I get a picture of you so I can show Santa what I want for Christmas?' It works best around Christmas time, obviously, but a pickup line should always make a girl laugh. She's putty in your hand after that."

Max nodded, almost in awe.

Michelle shook her head. "Don't listen to him, Max. Pickup lines are worthless. Be yourself."

Max glanced from Michelle to Weston, trying to decide who to believe.

"Well you both dated Anna. How did you guys meet her?" I asked. "Not with a pickup line I hope."

Weston grinned. "She worked at the coffee shop around the corner from my firm. I asked her, 'Did the sun come up or did you smile at me?'"

Michelle and I groaned.

"And she bought that?" I asked.

Weston smirked. "Of course. I told you, pickup lines work."

"What about you Max? How did you meet Anna?"

Max looked uncomfortable. "I own a bakery and she called to cancel the order for her wedding cake. She was crying." He glanced over at Weston and Weston squirmed a little. Good. "I remembered her from when she'd come in to order it. We talked for a few minutes. She kept apologizing for the inconvenience and apologizing for crying and I kept telling her it was fine. And then I ran into her a week later at the grocery store. We discovered we lived in the same neighborhood and she invited me over for dinner. We only dated for a few weeks. She wasn't ready for another serious relationship."

Michelle and I exchanged looks. Max was such a better catch. Anna must be blind to still be in love with Weston. Maybe she'd come to her senses after watching this on TV later.

Greg clapped his hands together. "Okay, let's hear the next conversation starter, shall we?"

Michelle picked hers up and read. "What is the craziest thing you've ever done?"

"That's an easy one for me," Max said. "Opening up my own bakery. My parents were sure it was going to be a disaster, but they helped finance it anyway. The best day of my life was the day I paid back the last of their seed money."

Weston smirked. "Well, the craziest thing I ever did was get engaged. I don't believe in marriage. I told Anna that after we'd been dating for six months and she freaked out and threatened to break up with me. We both got emotional and the next thing I knew I was asking her to marry me. I wanted to take it back the second I said it, but she was so happy that I went with it. But I never wanted to get married. Once she realized how miserable I was, she broke off the engagement. If I ever marry, it will be when I'm old and need someone to take care of me."

"How about dessert?" Michelle asked, eager to keep Weston from continuing his blather. I jumped up with her to dish out the ice cream and the guys gathered up the plates and forks and started washing and drying dishes.

When we were done with our dessert we sat down together on the couches and played Pictionary. It was a favorite game of mine, but Max couldn't draw and Michelle was a terrible guesser. The un-dynamic duo. Not that I minded being on the winning team, but Weston felt the need to revel in it. A lot.

I was about to suggest a different game when I caught movement in the Dave/Greg camp. They were discussing something, strategizing, if their body language was any indication. They caught me looking at them and Dave shooed me back to the game. He didn't want it to look like I was bored with the date, even if I was.

A minute later an assistant came into the apartment holding a small animal carrier under her arm. No one else noticed. They were busy studying Max's stick figure he kept frantically jabbing with his pen. On Dave's signal, the assistant stooped down and opened the animal carrier, releasing a tiny field mouse. It streaked across the carpet, and hid under Michelle's thigh, before speeding under the couch.

The bloodcurdling scream that followed was probably Director Dave's finest moment. I didn't get to see his reaction though, because all eyes were on Michelle, including mine. She fell forward from her cross-legged position and shot up off the floor in a panic.

"Is it off? Is it off? Where is it?" Michelle raked her hands through her hair and down her arms and legs, over and over again.

Max stared at her as if she were possessed. "Where is what?"

"The mouse. Oh, there's a mouse in here! I hate these dumpy apartments. It's probably been through the kitchen, running across the food. Oh, ew!" Michelle shivered and glanced behind her, as if the poor thing was going to attack her from behind.

I wanted to reassure her, but I knew her reaction was exactly what the show was going for and I didn't want them to make us do it again. Instead, I ran to the kitchen and grabbed a broom. Weston held his hand out. "Allow me."

"Weston," I warned, dropping my voice. "You do not want to bash a mouse on camera. I was going to try to coax it outside."

"Good call. Okay, I'm going to lift the couch, and you stand here and sweep it towards the door.

Weston counted down and then lifted the couch. The mouse took off right for me, but then shot to my left and scurried down the hall and into the bathroom. Michelle wailed.

"I guess we know what Michelle's afraid of," Weston joked.

Michelle glared at him and backed into a corner of the living room. "Get the mouse out of here right now!" She'd finally put two and two together, noticing the animal carrier in the assistant's hand. She turned and glared at Dave. "How did you know?"

Dave shrugged, obviously proud of himself for exploiting her secret fear. He had them stop filming while they got the mouse back into the carrier and gave us a few minutes to calm down before starting again. The overturned Pictionary cards were strewn all over the floor and I bent to clean them up. Weston helped me, but he couldn't stop laughing.

"That was awesome," he whispered. "I can't believe the mouse went straight for her. Dave looks so proud."

I glanced back at Dave. Weston was right. Dave was trying to keep a smug grin from crossing his disgusting unshaven face as he reviewed the footage with a cameraman. Michelle came over and I gave her a hug.

"Don't give him the satisfaction," I whispered. "Act like it never happened."

She nodded and took a deep breath. "Okay. I can do this."

They took a few more minutes to film us wrapping up the date and talking about the mouse, pretending we didn't know how it got into the apartment.

Then Weston walked me to my apartment door. We chatted for a few minutes and he did a cruel, but hilarious impression of Michelle hopping up and down when the mouse ran under her. As our laughter died away Weston started leaning in with a hungry look in his eyes.

I put a warning hand on his chest. "What are you doing?"

"Saying goodnight." He smiled as if everything was perfectly normal and leaned in again, his lips brushing against my jaw. I pushed him back a little more firmly and retreated into my doorway.

"Come on, Bethany. You've gotta know I have a little crush on you."

"Weston, you said you don't believe in marriage. I do. I have zero interest in dating you."

Weston smiled at me, undeterred. "Let's not jump the gun here, babe. I'm attractive, you're attractive. Don't think any further ahead than that. Just answer this one little question: If I said you had a beautiful body, would you hold it against me?"

He started leaning in again, laughing at his own joke. Was he serious or acting? And was I supposed to respond as the real me or the acting me? I decided to go with the me that wanted this date to end.

"Good night Weston." I closed the door, barely missing his puckered lips.

Ten minutes later Michelle came in, a mysterious smile on her face.

"Please tell me Max didn't try to put any moves on you."

Michelle scoffed. "No, why?" Her eyes went wide. "Oh, no. Weston? Do you think Dave put him up to it?"

"No idea, but I didn't play along. This show is getting weirder and weirder."

Michelle yawned. "Yep, and think, tomorrow is only day three."

CHAPTER 9

The next morning, realizing where I was, I rolled over and groaned, mushing my face into the pillow. "I don't want to be here."

"Too late." Michelle grinned at me from the bathroom door. "You're stuck here, just like me. Unless you can convince Weston, Carter and Tyson to not vote for you tonight. You're the belle of the ball."

"Yes, so lucky. I have three guys pretending to be in love with me." I studied her for a minute. "Why did you say we're both stuck here? Can I ask about Patrick yet? Or is the topic still off limits?"

Michelle looked pensive. "After the prank I pulled on him in college, we never talked again—until now. He lives in New Jersey and I live in Colorado. If we want to have time to get to know each other again, it has to be here."

"Well I'm glad this show is good for something." I got up and started making my bed. "How did you and Patrick meet?"

"He was my algebra tutor. I had to pass algebra with at least a C and I was failing. He was patient with me and completely professional. He never talked about anything other than math. But I could tell he liked me, so after a while I went out of my way to be totally unprofessional during our tutoring sessions. He wouldn't respond to my flirting, so I finally sat on his lap and put my arms around his neck and told him I wasn't getting off until he asked me out." She smiled at the memory, but then her face got sad. "I was a big idiot back then. I didn't take anything seriously, including relationships."

She didn't say anything else and I didn't think I should press, so I got up and took my turn in the bathroom, which was already a jungle of cords, creams, makeup and hair products. There was no room for anything. Michelle and I decided after the first day that if the show wanted to film us being messy we'd let them.

***

Dave didn't have anything pressing for us to do that morning, as he was focusing all his attention on filming Eddie and Gretchen rubbing suntan lotion on each other and Jade and Marco splashing each other in the pool.

Weston tried to corner me as I was about to descend the stairs, but Anna came up behind us and I hurried down and claimed a pool chair next to Max. He was reading a book on business startups and I took the opportunity to ask him about his bakery. He patiently answered all my questions, but I could tell he was distracted so I opened my book and let him get back to his.

"Did Michelle say anything after the date last night?" Max asked me suddenly.

I turned to look at him. "What do you mean? She said she had a good time, except for the mouse, of course."

"Oh, nothing. I just wondered what she thought…of me." He blushed and I froze. It never occurred to me Max might have feelings for someone other than Anna. How awkward. Something must have registered in my face because he started back-pedaling. "I'm looking for feedback on how I am in social situations. That's all. It's nothing personal. I promise."

I wanted to reassure him before he had a panic attack, but I wasn't sure if I was allowed to tell him about Michelle and Patrick.

"Never mind. Pretend we never had this conversation. Please." His anxiety was rising with every second I delayed answering.

"Max. I won't say a word to Michelle. Because, she's a little preoccupied with someone else. I'm so sorry."

"Oh."

"She doesn't want it on the radar though." I motioned toward the cameras.

Max sighed. "I put my whole life on hold to come here. I'm letting my manager run the bakery for a month and I can't even check in with him. I thought it would be worth it if I found the love of my life here."

"Max, even if no one here is right for you, when you go home your bakery is going to be swarmed with women who want to meet you and it's going to be good for your business and good for your love life. Do you believe me?"

"No, but keep saying it. It's good for my ego, too." He smiled and I grinned back. Somewhere there was a girl out there that was going to be perfect for him. Somewhere far, far away from this dumpy apartment complex and its fake love triangles.

***

Not that I had anywhere to go, but knowing we were not allowed to leave the apartment complex or call home left me cagier than I expected. After changing out of my swimsuit, I took a walk around the perimeter of the apartment complex and on my second lap I ran into Carter and Holly coming from the other direction. They had been talking up a storm until they reached me. And then nothing. Holly pulled on Carter's arm as we reached the stairs, but he waved her off and kept walking with me. For a few seconds I thought she'd change her mind and dash after us, but she huffed her way up the stairs, turning to give me one last dirty look.

As I expected, Carter wanted to know if I was still game to hit up Dave about piano lessons. Holly had nothing to worry about. Carter wasn't interested in me and I had no reason for the twinge of disappointment I felt. Carter had been perfectly upfront with me about his motive for coming on the show and love was not a factor.

Get over it, Bethany.

We found Dave wrapping up an interview by the pool and presented our idea. Loving it, he immediately gathered a crew to follow us over to the piano in the conference room.

When we flipped on the lights I got a pretty good idea of where things stood for some of the other contestants. Sylvie and Eddie jumped apart from the corner of the conference room where they had been hiding and Dave frantically motioned at the cameramen, as if they didn't already have their cameras trained on the embarrassed couple.

"We'll take this somewhere else," Eddie mumbled, red-faced.

Sylvie clung to his arm and they fled out of the room. Dave sent a cameraman after them. Eddie had been wrapped around Gretchen that morning so I knew he was in deep trouble, at least with her. Devious Sylvie. I bet she'd never had any interest in Todd. It was all an act to get her ex jealous. And it worked. Eddie came back like a boomerang.

Dave looked torn between staying to film us and following after them. Carter and I headed over to the piano, but Dave immediately forbid it. "You two stay away from the piano until I get back. I don't even want you talking to each other. Bethany, why don't you come with me? I might need you to soothe Todd after he finds out about Sylvie."

"No!" Carter and I protested in unison. I looked at Carter. There was no way I was doing any Todd soothing, but my heart fluttered a little to see him bothered by the suggestion.

Dave rolled his eyes. "Bethany, this isn't much to ask. You dated him before, you couldn't show him a little sympathy for a few minutes? Preferably from a good camera angle?"

I wanted to tell Dave exactly what I thought of his suggestion, but Greg stepped between us and motioned for Dave to go before Carter or I got our hands on him.

"Bethany dear, come along with me. We're losing time now, and no one will make you do anything you're not comfortable with. And then we can get back to this lovely piano lesson of yours, okay?"

I was starting to see why Dave hired Greg to host this show.

Reluctantly, I followed Greg back up to the apartments where Sylvie and Gretchen were in the middle of a catfight. We missed the part where Gretchen found out about Eddie and Sylvie, but from the yelling and screaming I pieced together that the cameramen had guided Gretchen over to Sylvie and Eddie's new hiding spot so she could discover them.

Another cameraman came around the corner trailing Todd, who had also clearly been led into this mess.

"What's going on?" he asked, trying to suppress a grin. Stupid Todd, he thought he was here to help calm down hormonal women.

Sylvie took one look at Todd and burst into a fresh batch of tears. "I'm sorry!" she blubbered, before running into her apartment and slamming the door.

Todd turned to Gretchen and she snarled at him. "Don't you know anything? She doesn't care about you. She doesn't care about me. She only cares about herself!"

She ran down the corridor to the stairs, trying to ditch the cameras. Todd shrugged and turned to stare at Sylvie's closed door, indecision playing across his face.

Dave was trying to make eye contact with me, but I studiously avoided his gaze.

And then Todd turned and looked at me all on his own. Oh snap. I was not counting on that. "What are you doing here?" he asked.

"I...I heard the commotion," I mumbled lamely.

"Well, this obviously doesn't concern you so you can go back to your room." And there was the Todd I knew. Todd turned back to Sylvie's door and started tapping lightly.

"Sylvie, baby? It's me Todd. Can I come in? What's the matter, sweetheart?"

Well, I'd done my part. I walked back down to the conference room. Dave followed a few minutes later, an evil grin plastered across his face. He'd milked the situation for everything it could give and couldn't ask for more.

Carter glanced at me anxiously and I rolled my eyes, indicating he had nothing to worry about. Even if I'd been delirious and decided to go along with Dave's original idea, Todd had no interest in being consoled, at least by me.

When Dave gave us the go-ahead I followed Carter over to the small piano bench and sat down. Carter started to grab a folding chair and Dave interrupted. "What are you doing? Why aren't you sitting on the bench with her?"

"She needs to sit in front of middle c."

Dave sighed, as if to indicate actual learning was so low on his priority list. "You're trim people. Sit together. She can reach over you for middle c." He laughed at his little joke and then motioned for us to get started.

Carter didn't have a piano book so we worked off of what he had written down. He showed me how the notes on the page corresponded with the keys on the piano and I fumbled through some basic scales he'd written for me until they sounded smooth. I was concentrating so hard on the notes, I almost forgot about the cameras.

Dave interrupted again. "Carter, this is boring. We need you to act less like a stodgy piano teacher and more like a man."

"Excuse me?" Carter swung around on the piano bench to face Dave. "How am I not being a man?"

Dave glared back and continued. "I need you to lean into Bethany like maybe she doesn't have cooties and quit lecturing her on posture."

"Yeah, I got this." Carter swiveled back around and moved into me, putting his arms around my waist. Any concentration I had went out the window.

"Okay, play the scale one more time," he whispered in my ear. Scale? What was that again? He rested his chin on my shoulder and nuzzled my neck. I closed my eyes. Was it possible to feel every nerve in my body at the same time? "What's the matter Bethany?" he teased. "Go ahead and play it."

I wanted to pinch him, but my hands wouldn't obey me. They were frozen over the piano. "Stop it, jerk." I whispered back.

He laughed, his breath tickling my neck. "Stop what? I'm just trying to be a man."

I fumbled through the scale, hitting more notes wrong than right.

"That was excellent, Bethany," Carter said.

I elbowed him in the ribs and squirmed when he tickled mine. Then he picked up my hands and guided them through a jazzy version of "Mary Had a Little Lamb." We went on to play "Peter Peter Pumpkin Eater" and "The Muffin Man" before Dave got irritated and ordered Carter to play something romantic. Carter started playing Celine Dion's "My Heart Will Go On" while swaying us side to side. Needless to say, it took a while before Dave was satisfied.

As we were leaving, Carter asked about getting piano books. Dave looked skeptical. "If we're going to continue with this piano lesson storyline, I would need you to pump up the romance angle. I'm not getting enough chemistry between the two of you."

Carter sighed and I felt myself dying inside a little. I'd felt it, but maybe it was just me. Even Dave saw nothing there. Carter thought I was fun to goof around with, but that was it. Unrequited crushes are the worst. My best bet was to never let Carter know I liked him. But it was probably too late, even for that.

CHAPTER 10

I was hoping for a break after the piano lesson, but Dave told me I had thirty minutes to get my hair and makeup done and meet back by the pool in a swimsuit. He dismissed Carter with a shooing motion, telling him to go chat with the other lady contestants.

Dave and Greg had Tyson waiting for me down by the pool. Tyson smiled at me and shrugged. It looked like he hadn't been filled in on the details either.

"Okay, you two. I am looking for some fireworks today. Bethany, you've been playing coy with both Carter and Weston. I want you to make something happen here with Tyson. Tyson, put your best moves on Bethany and let's see some magic!" Dave grinned at me and then he and Greg backed away to watch from behind the cameras. I sighed and glanced over at Tyson. He wiggled his eyebrows at me and I burst into giggles. This was so ridiculous.

"Wait. Wait." I motioned for Dave and Greg to come back over. "We're on day three. What is the huge rush here?"

Greg glanced at Dave and Dave nodded. I knew I was about to get a completely PC answer from Greg.

"Bethany, we are exploring all avenues—"

"Stop," I interrupted. "I want an answer from Dave. I barely know Tyson. Why can't this wait until we've spent more time together?"

Dave sighed and rolled his eyes. "Bethany, this is a huge opportunity for you. We selected you from thousands of contestants looking for love. You signed a contract to see this through. I would hope in the future you won't question everything, but just this once I will give you an explanation."

If he was hoping to make me feel guilty, he was dreaming.

"Until we get this to a test audience, we won't know who America connects with. You could be voted off tonight and we want to make sure we have enough footage to satisfy their curiosity. One of you could get sick, the apartment building could collapse, we could have our funding pulled, a flock of zombie parrots could fly through and take us all out. What I'm trying to say is that I. Want. This. Now. Understood?"

"Fine." I collapsed onto one of the pool deck chairs they'd pulled together for us and motioned for Tyson to lounge next to me.

He curled up by my side and eyed me carefully. "If I drape my arm around your waist will I get it back in one piece?"

"I'm not mad at *you*," I whispered. I took his arm and put it around me. In a strange way, it was comforting to have him near.

"Enunciate," Dave commanded. "We want to catch all the flirty things you say to each other."

Tyson sat up and pulled off his sunglasses. "Dave, you're really killing the mood here. Can we have fewer interruptions?"

I had to smother a laugh. Dave actually looked apologetic. He stepped back and motioned for us to continue.

Tyson took the lead. He told me how beautiful I was and I smiled and stared into his eyes. He told me I made being on this show worthwhile, that I was funny, sweet, and sexy. He was good at this. Okay, this was manageable. Until I noticed Carter pacing in the background. Why was he hovering? Was he afraid I wouldn't want to continue piano lessons if I got distracted by Tyson? I didn't want to get my hopes up that he might actually be jealous.

I checked again. Carter was definitely watching us, although he was also half-listening to Gretchen and Holly. Holly was in a bikini even tinier than mine and her eyes never left Carter's face. Any time he moved she'd shift her body to be in front of him, like she was intent on positioning herself where he would have no choice but to notice her. She flipped back her hair and adjusted her swimsuit almost as if she were checking her reflection in a mirror, and the mirror was in his eyes. Only he never saw her. Carter's eyes would light on me, and then flit to Gretchen and nod in response to something she said, and then flit around to nothing in particular and then back at me. It was as if Holly was invisible. What was the deal with them?

"Earth to Bethany. I've been nibbling on your ear and all you do is stare at Carter. I see where I stand."

I pulled my eyes away and looked at Tyson. Busted. He was staring at me with his arms folded. "I'm not a jealous man, but even I have my limits. You don't see me when he's around."

"That's not true."

"Sure it is. And it's the same for him. Watch this." Tyson pulled me into him and started kissing me. He was a good kisser, but despite wanting to prove him wrong, I couldn't pay attention, knowing Carter could see us. Tyson was right.

I finally pulled away and we both looked over at Carter. His eyes met mine and the expression on his face was…frustrated.

"I'm sorry Tyson. I have to go."

I got to my feet and walked off in the other direction, ignoring Dave and Greg's protests and the cameraman trailing after me. I felt so humiliated, though I couldn't have explained why if someone asked me. This was my job. I was supposed to create romance for viewers. Why was it so hard?

Michelle wasn't in the apartment, thankfully. I needed time to sort out my feelings. Why did I have to have feelings for Carter? I could confront him. Ask him if he was playing with me. But that was insane. I didn't want to seem needy or insecure and I couldn't imagine it sounding any other way. And putting him in a situation where he might lie to me to spare my feelings, or worse, make a scene for better ratings. What would that solve?

Maybe I should ask Tyson not to vote for me tonight. I could go home. Back to my ordinary life and not worry about any of this. But this was about finding adventure and romance. Or die trying. Well, maybe not die. Although I could stage a small accident for Director Dave. I smiled at the thought.

I searched the apartment, looking for chocolate. If I was going to wallow, I needed something to munch on. Ooh, Snickers. How did these not get eaten already?

Even with the chocolate, I couldn't get the feeling of Carter pressed up against me on the piano bench out of my mind. Was he even considering voting for me? I didn't want to let that thought in, but it wedged its way into my brain anyway and camped there.

He's probably voting for Holly. Not that it mattered. Dang Carter. I could still smell his aftershave on my neck.

***

To start off elimination night, we had a poolside cocktail party. The brightly-colored spotlights shining across the water and cozily arranged patio furniture were a nice touch, but there was no food, just lots of booze. A slightly drunk Todd came up to me for some last minute kissing up. Now that Sylvie wasn't interested, I was his next best option.

"Bethany. You look so beautiful. I mean that. I really do. I really do think…." He paused stupidly. "You…you look beautiful. I mean it."

He was too drunk to realize the more he tried to reassure me of his sincerity, the less sincere he sounded.

"Thanks, Todd. It's always been my dream to attend a cocktail party in a zebra-print polyester dress that bunches around my hips."

He laughed loudly and punched me in the arm. "You're such a sport. Sport."

Carter came over and pulled me away. "You don't have to put up with that. Walk away next time."

"I know, Carter." I was irritated that he was telling me how to handle my ex. And even less mature, I was mad at him for constantly being on my mind.

We went and sat together on one of the 'conversation benches' the show set up to look private and cozy. I stared up at the cheap plastic ficus trees filled with twinkling lights. Carter shook the ice in his glass nervously and cleared his throat. "Are you mad at me?" he asked.

I shook my head, too aware of the cameras. "It's nothing."

Carter put his hand out as if to cover mine but then withdrew it at the last second and gripped the edge of the bench instead. "Bethany I—"

Holly came around the fake shrubbery right then and scooted in next to Carter. "You don't mind if I squeeze in do you?" She gave me her most insincere smile and stole Carter's drink, crunching down on a piece of ice. I steeled myself to respond with complete indifference, and sneaking a glance at Carter, knew he had decided to go the same route. He stared ahead as if we were three strangers at a bus stop.

Greg tinged his glass to get our attention and then motioned us into the conference room, where they had an ugly dining table set up with little white place cards. The table was one of those oversized, gaudy faux-Victorian monstrosities and all the chairs were mismatched. Someone must have scoured antique sales and flea markets for weeks to satisfy Dave's sick need to make everything on the show ugly.

I walked around until I found my name. I was on the end next to Michelle, and Tyson was across from us. He winked at me and leaned back in his wicker chair. His smile turned to a grimace as the chair gave way and Tyson's butt hit the floor.

Conveniently, a cameraman was trained on him, ready to catch the footage. I glanced up at Dave and saw that familiar smug smile. He couldn't help himself. Tyson was a goof and Dave, being Dave, had to keep pushing the idea until he was satisfied, which would be never.

Tyson picked himself up and tried to act like it was no big deal, but his face was red and he plastered on an uncomfortable smile. An assistant brought over a new chair and Tyson sat down carefully, keeping his arms on the table for support.

Once we were all seated, Greg launched into a long on-camera speech. We'd been instructed to hang on his every word, and I leaned forward and fixed what I hoped was a concentrated expression on my face.

"This is your moment!" he said, pointing at each one of us. "You get one vote to express your intentions. With this vote you choose who is most important to you here. Choose the person you want to spend more time with, the person you might even be starting to love. Don't worry about how anyone else votes, even if fighting for the same person will send someone else home. This is not the time to hide your feelings or worry about offending someone." His eyes blazed as he punctuated each sentence with a fist in the air. "Fight for the one you love! Dare to love and be loved!"

It was a stirring speech and I felt a little swell of pride for Greg. It was a little much for the show, but whatever Kool-Aid Greg was selling, I was buying. He could do commercials after this, maybe even get his own daytime talk show. I was so distracted, I forgot we were about to vote.

"Why don't we start over here with you, Todd?" Greg's toothy grin seemed over-large in the face of my sudden panic. Not Todd. Don't start with Todd. I'd been hoping they'd start with my end of the table and I could get my vote over with.

"Todd, who would you like to continue with you on this journey? Who do you vote for?"

Todd turned to me and I froze. *Don't say it. Don't say it.*

"I'd like Bethany to stay on the show with me. We've been through so much." He smiled at me in a way he thought looked sincere, but I knew meant he was trying too hard. I smiled back and then had to look away from his puppy dog eyes.

As much as Todd had hurt me, I'd never had any kind of revenge fantasy about hurting him back. And rejecting him in public like this was pretty much the only kind of hurt that mattered to him. But I couldn't vote for him. Even if I didn't have Tyson or Carter to consider, Todd couldn't be a part of my future, however temporary.

Sylvie was sitting across from Todd and Greg turned to her next. "Sylvie, who would you like by your side as you continue on this journey?"

Sylvie smiled shyly and picked Eddie.

Eddie picked Sylvie back. The two of them stared at each other like they wanted to climb over the table and into each other's arms. They did make quite a striking couple. Eddie, the tan, muscular blond, and Sylvie, the fair-skinned beauty with the shiny black curls.

Gretchen started to cry. It was her turn next and she picked Carter while shooting daggers at Sylvie with her eyes. A paler-than-usual Carter calmly picked Holly. He mouthed something apologetic to Gretchen, but she turned her head away and wouldn't look at him. Holly picked Carter as well, guaranteeing at least one guy was leaving.

Jada and Marco picked each other. No surprise there. Jada looked super annoyed with Gretchen's crying. Marco looked bored. I think they were both counting down the minutes until they could be done with this and run off to the hot tub.

Weston was next. He smiled at Anna. "I choose Bethany."

What? I looked up and glared at Weston. He winked at me. Ugh. What was he doing? And then I remembered. He never wanted Anna on this show in the first place. He wanted her voted off. I glanced at Anna. She stared blankly ahead, fiddling with her place card as if she didn't care. Maybe she didn't. But then her poker face started to leak. A big tear escaped and ran down her cheek.

Anna didn't say anything for a long time, staring at each of us in turn. Finally, she turned and glared at Weston. "I choose Weston." Weston narrowed his eyes at her and the ghost of a smile crossed her face. Maybe he didn't want her here, but she knew he didn't want to be here either. Now he had to stay at least another week before he could get back to being a fancy lawyer. I tried not to laugh.

Patrick chose Holly, mumbling something about wanting to get to know her better. Holly stared back at him like she'd as soon feed him to a crocodile.

Max didn't even pause when it was his turn. "I'd like Michelle by my side."

Michelle smiled at him sadly, but she didn't look surprised. I knew she'd been cooking up a way to keep her relationship with Patrick under the radar. She must have recruited Max to help.

Michelle tried to be very casual. "I choose Patrick. I feel like we left things unfinished and I'd like some closure with him."

I watched Dave's face, trying to gauge how much of it he was buying. Patrick was doing his best to look surprised, but he wasn't much of an actor.

My choice wasn't hard. Tyson put all his eggs in my basket and I owed him. And honestly I needed his friendship more than I wanted to admit. It was the only thing I knew was real at the moment. "I vote for Tyson."

Tyson smiled at me. "Right back at ya. I vote for Bethany. She's a total babe."

Gretchen started to get up, but Dave yelled for everyone to stay seated. "We've got to film goodbyes and parting interviews people. Everyone stay where you are. We won't feed you until we get this right."

We were all starving so we sat and waited for instructions. They let Todd go first. He got some awkward hugs and back pats from everyone, and then he approached me.

"This hurts Beth. I voted for you and you let me down." He went in for a hug and I forced myself not to recoil and hugged him back.

"Take care of yourself, Todd." I hoped this goodbye was forever. He seemed like he was about to say something else but luckily Max came up behind him and I threw myself into his arms. "I will miss you something fierce, Max."

"You will?" He blushed, trying not to look too pleased.

I laughed. "I will. You are a breath of fresh air. Leave here and don't look back. I'll come visit your bakery someday. Save me a dozen cookies."

"Okay."

Michelle came to stand next to me and I released Max so they could say their goodbyes. Carter hovered nearby. I refused to look at him directly, but I could see him with Holly on his arm, walking around in my periphery. If he wanted to talk to me he'd have to lose his arm-candy. The disappointment that he voted for Holly stung a little, although I wasn't surprised. They had a connection as clear as mud, but it was a connection. I wished I understood it.

I didn't hug Gretchen or Anna. I hadn't gotten to know them well enough for that. In Anna's case I wished I would have. She seemed nice, if a little clueless about men, but then aren't we all?

After they left to do their closing interviews, we sat back down and Greg poured us some champagne. They also brought in hot dogs and bags of potato chips on cheap paper plates in case things were getting too fancy. I was too hungry to care. I ate two hot dogs and a huge pile of chips.

CHAPTER 11

I woke up to Michelle fluttering something in my face. She was such a morning person; I couldn't stand it.

"What?" I wanted to tell her to kill the lights, but then realized it was the sun peeking in through a crack in the curtains. They were cute curtains. I opened my eyes fully and studied them. Old, but a nice paisley pattern. They'd make a cute skirt. Oh, who was I kidding? This wasn't *The Sound of Music*.

Michelle bounced on the edge of my bed. "We're still here and we have dates!" she sang.

"Why are you so excited about it?"

Her eyes flitted to the bedroom door and I looked over. Cameras. I was going to murder Michelle, right after I murdered Dave for filming me waking up.

"That's great!" I forced myself to say. "Do we know who our dates are yet?"

Michelle shook her head. "We'll find out soon. And it's one-on-one dates this time."

"That's great!" I said again. My brain was fuzzy. Michelle laughed at me and then shooed the cameramen out. She came back in, throwing a blanket over the curtains before heading to the shower, fully blocking out the sun. Okay, I guess I could forgive her. I rolled over and went back to sleep.

***

"I need a new pretend boyfriend now that Max is gone," Michelle said as we were eating breakfast.

"Poor Max. He liked you, you know."

Michelle shook her head. "I talked to him about it. He realized he was trying too hard to find love here. It was a relief for him to go home."

"So, you're going to continue to hide things with Patrick?" I asked.

"For as long as I can. Do you mind lending me one of your beaus? Tyson or Carter maybe?"

"What, you're not interested in Weston? Because I'll gladly send his admiration your way."

Michelle's shoulders slumped. "Yeah, he's probably my best option. Yuck."

Dave must have agreed, because he sent Weston over later in the morning to officially ask Michelle on a date. Weston didn't say hi or even look in my direction. So much for his crush on me.

Carter came a few minutes later to invite me on our date. I wondered if they told him to ask me out or if he got to choose. But I didn't want to dwell on doubts and pessimism. It wasn't every day I had a date with a hot guy.

And to my delight, we were going first. Dave told me to get dressed and meet Carter at the foot of the stairs at noon. I decided to rock a pair of yellow stirrup pants since I could hide the bottoms in tall boots. Paired with a long button down shirt, I almost looked normal...to a color-blind person with fuzzy eyesight.

Carter was waiting for me with two long drivers and a bucket of golf balls. He held them out like a gift. "Since you golf, I thought we could hit some off the roof."

"Cool! Where did you get those?" I asked.

"You're not supposed to ask," he murmured in my ear. "It's the magic of TV."

"I do love to golf," I said loudly. Carter chuckled and I turned red. So much for acting. I tried to concentrate on Carter's face and forget about the cameras.

"I can't golf," Carter admitted. "Not that I've had much practice. I've golfed maybe twice."

"I can't golf either."

71

"Then what are we doing with these?" Carter whispered. "Dave assured me you were a golfer. He wanted you to…you know…help me with my swing." He hit an imaginary ball and winked at me.

I laughed. "I can pretend to help you with your swing. I like golf. I do. But I'm terrible at it. I only go in the summer when they slash the rates and the courses are empty. That way we can take our time and there aren't any angry retired guys waiting behind us. I haven't gone in a while though. My golfing buddy is expecting. Triple digit heat and flying golf balls aren't usually recommended for pregnant ladies."

"Ah, Phoenix in summer. I'm so sorry I'm missing that," he said sarcastically.

"The discounted golf makes it totally worth it. And did I mention we have the best freeway system in the United States?"

"We don't need freeways in Minot. No traffic. And it's green and open, and we have rivers."

"That flood," I pointed out. We continued to tease each other all the way up to the roof. I'm pretty sure our camera guy was super annoyed with us, which made it even more fun.

The crew had a little platform in the southwest corner all set up with Astroturf for us. More of the magic of TV, I assumed. Carter motioned for me to go first. I placed my ball on the tee and then stared out into the distance at the scrubby desert dotted with the occasional Joshua tree and not much else. I noticed they'd set us up on the picturesque side where you couldn't see the highway and the trailer park communities in the distance. I gave the ball a good whack and I watched it arch up and out and make a little dirt cloud before rolling to a stop.

It was time for Carter to take his turn, but he seemed to be frozen, staring over the edge like it might come to get him. He climbed up next to me, but only looked more freaked out. I laid my driver down and wrapped my arms around him, hoping all the camera would see was a cheesy hug.

"What is it?" I whispered into his chest. "Your golf swing can't be that terrible."

"I don't like heights. I didn't think it would be this bad. But the wind is whipping us all over the place and the edge is—right there." He closed his eyes and started to sway a little. If this wasn't potentially humiliating for him, I would have thought it was an act.

I'd never encountered anyone this afraid of heights before.

"Open your eyes and look at me," I commanded. Carter blinked and then focused on my face. "Take this driver and hit the ball. Only look at the ball. I'm going to spoon you from behind like a desperate German shepherd and then we'll get off this roof and go do something else. Okay?"

"Okay." Carter slowly turned to the side so he could swing at the ball and I edged around him until I was holding him from behind. His first swing was wild and he missed the ball completely. He swore under his breath and I couldn't help laughing a little.

"Sorry," I whispered.

"I got this," he said, I think more to convince himself than to convince me. He took a deep breath and tried again. His driver connected with the golf ball, but it didn't go high enough to clear the roof. The ball nipped the top edge and bounced back, hitting an air conditioning unit with a loud clang.

I snickered and Carter looked back at me, red faced. "Dang it all, I have to do this again?" He was trying to be mad about it, but he was laughing.

"Afraid so." I put down another golf ball and then stood up and put my hands on his shoulders. His body was so tense, I stopped him before he could try to swing again. "Loosen up a little." I rubbed his shoulders and felt a little of the tension leave him. "Are you ready?"

"I think I need you to rub my shoulders a little more." I poked him in the ribs. "All right, all right. I'm ready."

He took a deep breath and hit the ball as hard as he could. It sailed off the roof and Carter didn't wait to see where it landed. He grabbed my hand and pulled me off the platform with him, letting out all the air he'd been holding in.

"Sorry about that," he whispered. "I purposely avoided anything in my interviews or on my application about my fear of heights, but I bet Holly told them. Dave was the one to suggest the roof."

"Why would Holly tell him?"

I could see a fleeting moment of panic in Carter's face before he went back to normal. "Because she's crazy. I don't know." He glanced over at the cameras, looking worried.

I decided not to press him. Now wasn't the time, but eventually I wanted to know what he was hiding about her.

"You're not afraid of heights?" he asked as we walked back downstairs.

"A little. But after bungee jumping, this was a piece of cake."

"You went bungee jumping?" Carter looked at me as if I'd just admitted I played Russian roulette with drug addicts for fun.

"Yeah. My friend Katelyn, you know, my golfing buddy, we have the same birthday, so every year we do something we've never tried before on our birthday together. When we turned eighteen we went bungee jumping."

"What was it like?"

"Choosing to step off the edge of the platform, that's probably the hardest part. Then you're falling and you think you're going to die, but that heart-in-your-throat feeling only lasts for a few seconds. And then you still have all that adrenaline pumping through you. It feels awesome, the wind whipping in your ears, the amazing view."

"That's cool you do something new every year. What other things have you done?"

Suddenly, all I could think of was the wet T-shirt contest of three years ago. It was the stupidest thing she'd ever come up with, except for the fact Katelyn met her husband there and now they were starting a family. Why was it when Katelyn tried crazy things, everything came up roses? All I got from the wet T-shirt contest was nightmares about photos showing up on the internet and a couple of skeevy guy's phone numbers.

"Cat got your tongue?" Carter asked, smiling.

"No, just reminiscing. Last year we learned how to tango."

"The tango, huh? I'm more of a salsa guy myself."

"Really?" I smiled, thinking how much I'd like to see him salsa.

"No, not really." He laughed. "I dance about as well as I golf."

"No way. You're a musician. You've gotta be a dancer."

Carter took my hands and laced them around his neck. "I can slow dance like this, in a circle. Maybe add a little sway." He put his hands on my waist and swayed us side to side. "And if I stare into your eyes and whisper sweet nothings, you might not notice when I step on your feet."

His eyes had a mischievous gleam to them, probably because he knew his plan would totally work on someone like me. Someone so enamored with him that she couldn't think straight. He smiled at me and I shook my head and smiled back, knowing my face was growing redder every second. A part of me was loving this, but the other part wanted to run away before I felt too much.

"But if you took lessons I bet you'd be a good dancer," I blurted out.

Carter shrugged. "I can't imagine going to dancing lessons unless a girl dragged me there. Dancing's not much fun without a good partner."

His eyes locked on mine and the pressure of his hands on my hips was doing funny things to my brain.

"Speaking of lessons," I said, reluctantly letting my hands drop from around his neck, "we should end our date with another piano lesson."

***

We worked on rhythm this time, with Carter explaining measures and beats. I felt dumb when he made me clap out the beat, but he clapped with me and I did my best to pretend the cameras weren't there. And then I made Carter play for me. I made sure to ask him about his music and he told me all about it as if we'd never had the conversation before. I rested my head on his shoulder while he played, not caring if he thought it was for the cameras. The piano music was soothing and feeling his relaxed concentration was strangely mesmerizing. I didn't want him to ever stop, but eventually he did.

"Do you give piano lessons at home?" I asked.

Carter shook his head. "I run an after-school music program during the school year, but private lessons, no. There are two ladies in my town everyone takes lessons from. One is my former piano teacher. She's in her 70s but has no desire to retire any time soon."

"You could do online lessons, you know. With Skype or YouTube videos."

"I'd never thought of that before." He glanced over at the cameras with a thoughtful look on his face and I knew what he was thinking. This little bit of celebrity might open up all sorts of avenues for him. For all of us.

My stomach clenched at the thought. Being here was crazy, but going home might not be any easier. However fleeting, I didn't look forward to being a celebrity, especially with my boss exploiting it.

I looked up and caught Carter staring at me.

"What?"

"Nothing."

He looked down at his hands before restlessly running them across the piano, letting out a chaotic and melancholy tune.

"That sounds dramatic."

He stopped playing and smiled at me. "I'll call it Jealousy in A Minor."

I laughed uncomfortably and he turned red. "Sorry. Choir jokes are lame. Ask my students."

What was he talking about? Jealousy? Maybe he was just teasing me.

The confusion must have shown on my face.

"Sometimes it's hard not to get sucked into all this…this dating stuff. The love triangles and all that."

I glanced at the cameras and realized he was not going to spell it out for me. Was he jealous of me and Tyson? He had to know it was fake.

Dave came in to let us know we should wrap up our date so he could lock up the conference room. Maybe he was trying to keep Eddie and Sylvie from sneaking back here.

The cameras and crew led us back to my door where Carter and I stood together awkwardly.

"I had a really nice time today," I offered lamely.

"Yeah, me too."

He tucked a strand of hair behind my ear and let his hand linger there. In every normal scenario it would be a signal that I should lift my head so he could kiss me, but I stared at my toes, frozen by insecurity. I didn't know if he had real feelings for me, or a bit of real mixed with fake, or if all of it was fake, and until I knew I felt lost.

Carter lifted my chin and looked me in the eyes. "I'm so glad to know you, Bethany." He kissed my forehead and then walked off. It was just enough and not too much. I ran in my door and locked it before Dave could protest and make us do it his way.

CHAPTER 12

Michelle's date started right after mine, so I didn't see her again until that night when I returned from a jog. She was sitting on the couch watching a rerun of *Saved by the Bell*. I was all over that, but I needed something to keep my hands busy, and not make me feel like I was wasting the rest of the evening. I'd bet ten bucks there were twelve encore episodes after this one and we would probably sit here and watch all of them unless we were dragged off for interviews.

After my shower, I went to the closet and found a skirt shaped like a sack and brought it back to the couch with our contraband supplies. Michelle had decided not to ask Dave about a sewing machine and instead, buttered up to a young, very smitten assistant and got him to smuggle us a travel-sized sewing kit.

Michelle looked over. "Oh, nice choice."

I tried it on and pinched the sides, safety-pinning the excess material that was about to go bye-bye. I wished I'd paid more attention in Home Economics class. My hope was this was going to end up looking like a pencil skirt.

"How was your date?" Michelle asked.

"Fine. How about yours?"

"Weston and I had a picnic lunch. It would have been really nice with a set of ear plugs. He told me way more than I ever wanted to know about his law firm, his apartment, his past girlfriends, blah, blah, blah. And then at the end of the date he said he was falling in love with me and thought we could be good together, you know, for a while."

I laughed. "Very persuasive."

"I told him I was studying to be a nun and took a vow of celibacy. He told me that sounded like a challenge, and then I shut the door in his face."

"Wow. Sadly, none of that surprises me."

"He might be acting, but if he is, he's really good at playing a jerk."

"Too good," I agreed.

We went back to watching *Saved by the Bell* and I got to work with the seam ripper and tiny scissors. On TV, Mr. Belding was warning Zack and Slater not to prank a rival school and I glanced over at Michelle while we watched. She caught me looking at her and rolled her eyes.

"You're wondering about it, aren't you?" she said, flipping off the TV.

"Wondering about what?" It was better to pretend I didn't know what she was talking about.

"How Patrick and I broke up in college."

"Maybe a little. So what happened?"

Michelle let out a big sigh and paused the TV. "I hate telling this story. It makes me look bad." She stared at me for a minute. Probably wondering why she was about to tell me. But I could tell she was ready to spill it, so I waited.

"They had this stupid thing called prank week at our school. They gave out spirit points for good pranks, and the more embarrassing and public they were, the better. Patrick and I had been dating for a few months, and a friend of mine gave me an ultrasound picture she took from work. In retrospect, that was totally unprofessional of her, but that's not the point. She suggested I show it to Patrick and say it was mine."

"An ultrasound, like a pregnancy ultrasound?" I asked.

Michelle squirmed. "Yes. And being totally stupid, I thought it was a great idea and wanted to get a whole lot of spirit points, so I told a bunch of people I was pulling a prank on Patrick on the quad, and I asked him to meet me there. I showed him the picture with all these people around us pretending they weren't watching. I don't know what I expected his reaction to be. I doubt I gave it a lot of thought. Anyway, he stood very quietly looking at it, and then he hugged me and told me he loved me and he'd marry me if that's what I wanted. I didn't know what to do. There was this horrible weight on my chest, like I couldn't breathe. How do you say just kidding to that? But then I didn't need to because some guy shouted out, 'Look, they gave birth to a prank!'

"Everyone started laughing, and Patrick looked at me, and then down at the ultrasound picture. He threw it on the ground and walked off. I ran after him, calling his name, but he only ran faster and I tripped and skinned my knee with all those people watching, and he didn't even turn around. He just kept going. That was the end of our relationship. I was broken-hearted, but too stubborn to admit it. He's since told me he felt the same way."

"Oh that's awful." I stared down at my sewing project, concentrating on my fingers. I was afraid my face would show sympathy, or shock, or amusement, all of which I was feeling. What a story. Poor Michelle. And poor Patrick.

"I thought I was over him, but when they said they had our exes on the show, I wasn't mad. I was hoping it was Patrick. Even if it means Dave digs up this story and tells everyone in America. All my relationships since Patrick have been filler. He was the one that got away."

***

The next morning I hit the gym early. I've never liked exercise. For me, it's a necessary evil, like eating broccoli. Katelyn and I ran a 10k on our twenty-fourth birthday. I'd made Katelyn leave me behind after she started jogging backwards and shouting encouragement. She finished middle of the pack. I came in 957th place. And that was after training for six months.

But being stuck in this apartment complex makes the tiny gym on the bottom floor seem like an oasis, and I've been getting pretty attached to it. Unfortunately, so have the other contestants. I usually wait until they're done so I'm not bumping elbows and having to make conversation while sweating.

Carter came in as I was starting my run on the treadmill. I flitted between worry that he would see me all sweaty and excitement he was here.

We smiled at each other, and then he sat down at the weight bench. The treadmills make it impossible to talk. They're ancient and loud, like jets taking off, loud. But even though we couldn't hear each other, my awareness of Carter was off the charts. It took all my concentration to stare at the numbers on the display in front of me. I didn't care how many calories I was burning or how far I'd gone, but if I didn't stare at those numbers I'd be staring at his bicep curls. And they were awesome. He obviously worked out regularly, I mean, you don't develop a body like his with just wishes.

Sneaking another glance, I almost tripped. Oops. It might be time to turn my speed down a notch. As I reached the one mile mark, I considered leaving. No need for him to catch onto my staring problem. But unrequited crush or not, I wanted to stay. We were alone together without cameras, or Holly. This was an opportunity I couldn't pass up.

I got off the treadmill and took my turn doing arm curls with the ten pound weights, the smallest I could find. Carter had moved on to sit ups and pushups. Who knew something that mundane could be so fascinating. Even the mix of sweat and spicy deodorant coming off his skin made my heart beat a little faster.

There were a million ways to start a conversation, but I couldn't find the words. And the longer I delayed, the more tongue-tied I felt.

He let out a last puff of air and crossed his arms over his knees, looking over at me. "Try to hold your elbows still," he said, watching my form.

I blushed. Of course he'd notice I was doing it wrong.

"Here," he came over and stood behind me, straightening my back. I jumped at his touch and he let go. "Sorry, it's the teacher in me. I should have asked if you wanted help."

Was I interested in perfect arm curls? No. Interested in Carter's attention? Yes. "It's okay. What am I doing wrong?"

He rolled my shoulders back and then ran his hand down my arm. "Keep your elbow tucked in right here and don't let it swing. Now bend your knees a little and plant your feet. Wait, spread them apart a little more."

I did as he asked, aware of his hands on my back, his breath on my neck and the rumbling sound of his voice in my ear.

"Okay, now try a curl."

Oops. I'd forgotten about the exercise. After a set of ten curls he stayed at my back, his fingers lightly touching my hips. Was this normal for personal trainers? It felt awfully personal. I switched arms, afraid he'd move away if I stopped. If there was ever a time to go for a new arm curl record it was now. I kept doing sets of ten on each side until my arms were ready to fall off. My heart felt like it was about to jump out of my chest, partially from the exercise.

"That's probably good." He stepped back and when I turned to look at him, he didn't meet my eyes. He ran his hands through his hair and let out a long breath.

"Are you okay?" I asked, wishing he hadn't moved away.

"Oh, yeah. I'm fine. You should stretch your arms and shoulders now." He backed up into the door, still not looking at me and then turned and left.

The room felt stuffy and dull without him in it. I'd felt something, an electricity in the air, and I knew he did, too. But he'd run away from it. Feeling frustrated, I did some halfhearted stretches and then packed up my things and left.

***

Dave and Greg pounced on me as I reached the door to my apartment. "We need you to take a shower."

I put my hand up. "I did not sign up for on-camera nudity."

Dave looked at the ceiling and sighed. "Why is she so difficult?" he asked Greg. Greg put his hands out in a placating way. "We're not filming you in the shower. We just need you to soap and rinse quickly, then put a bunch of shampoo in your hair, and wait before rinsing it off."

"Wait for what?"

Dave grinned. "You'll know when it happens." He handed me a fluffy bathrobe and walked off.

What was that supposed to mean? I worried about it all through my shower, glancing around with suspicion, even though Michelle assured me no one had been in there. After waiting in nervous boredom for five minutes with sudsy hair, the water trickled to a drip. There was no way I was leaving the bathroom undressed, even with a bathrobe, so after toweling off, I put my shorts and tank top back on before donning the bathrobe and wrapped my hair, now stiff with shampoo, in my towel.

Opening the door a crack, I glanced around and sure enough, I almost bumped into a cameraman standing against the wall. That's my cue, I thought.

"Michelle?" I hollered. "There's no water pressure. I still have shampoo in my hair."

Michelle came around the corner, studiously avoiding eye contact with the cameras. "I know. I was doing dishes and it suddenly stopped. Let's go see what's wrong."

Michelle was no actress. I could tell in the tone of her voice, and even in the way she walked to the door that she was not being her natural self. I followed her downstairs where Tyson and Carter were sitting in lawn chairs, filling up water balloons. A few other hoses snaked across the grass and up into a large rectangular inflatable pool that was almost filled.

I let out a big sigh. Really? They would have to do some serious editing to make this follow any sort of logical reasoning. Tyson approached me first.

"What's wrong Bethany?"

"There's no water upstairs. What are you guys doing?"

"We're getting ready for a pool party. Cool, huh."

Michelle came up behind me and glared at them with her hands on her hips. "You guys killed our water pressure and Bethany needs to wash the shampoo out of her hair."

"I'll do it," both guys chorused.

While they argued about who was going to have the honor of rinsing my hair, I glanced at Michelle and rolled my eyes. Besides not making sense plumbing-wise, this had to be the dumbest idea in the history of the universe. Pulling the towel off my head, I was about to grab one of the hoses and do it myself, but Carter stepped forward, pushing Tyson out of the way. I bent at the waist and let Carter run the hose over my head. I knew the water would be cold, but I did not expect every nerve in my head to react to Carter's fingers in my hair.

He gently massaged my scalp and whispered an apology for this ridiculous scheme. I suddenly was not nearly as annoyed with it as I had been previously. I hoped it would take him forever to get all the shampoo out. And then, bless her, Michelle handed over a bottle of conditioner and Carter rubbed it in, holding fistfuls of my hair up so it wouldn't drip down into my face. My neck was killing me but I hardly noticed as he softly towel dried my hair and then took my shoulders and helped me straighten back up.

"Thanks," I whispered.

He smiled at me, his eyes twinkling in amusement. For a second

I forgot where we were. At least until Director Dave interrupted, complaining my hair hadn't looked sudsy enough when I came down the stairs and I would need to reshoot that part.

An assistant brusquely rubbed a ridiculous amount of shampoo into my hair until there was enough visible lather to satisfy Dave. They carefully covered it back up with a towel, and warned me not to press down too much. Then Michelle and I tromped back up the stairs and came down again. We redid our conversation with Tyson and Carter, and then Carter once again won the chance to rinse my hair.

However, this time, Director Dave yelled cut right after Carter started rinsing and some assistant came over and quickly finished the job. The assistant handed me a wide-tooth comb and I got my now squeaky-clean hair into a quick bun as Dave was yelling new directions.

Jada and Marco were waiting upstairs for their cue to come down and yell about needing water, and then Tyson was instructed to strike Jada with a water balloon. Marco, defending her honor, would get in a shouting match with Tyson, then there would be a shove back and forth, and Tyson was supposed to fall backward into the kiddie pool. Tyson looked psyched. This was as close as he'd ever come to starring in an action movie.

Jada and Marco sauntered down the steps in their small swimwear and Jada complained about needing to wash off her suntan lotion. She turned to show her oiled back to the boys, Tyson's cue. He lobbed a big pink water balloon at her back, but it bounced off and splattered on the ground.

Worker bee assistants quickly picked up water balloon pieces and wiped off Jada's legs and then they tried it again, and again, and again. Finally, an assistant pushed a pin through the back of Jada's swimsuit and after three more tries, Tyson's balloon struck the right spot. The balloon exploded all over her and she roared in fake indignation.

Marco ran down the steps and chased Tyson around the little swimming pool, finally picking him up and throwing him into it. So much for Dave's directions. Dave liked his improvisation, but had them dry off and do it again four more times. An assistant was actually assigned to blow dry and towel off Tyson's swimming trunks every time.

Michelle and I were having such a good time watching, I didn't notice Carter sneak up behind me with a water balloon. I gasped as a gush of water ran down my neck and I turned and caught him, tackling him to the ground. He hit his head pretty hard when we landed and I leaned over him, afraid he was hurt. Carter closed his eyes and moaned, but when I hovered over his face, he took another water balloon and broke it over my head.

The nerve! "Where are you hiding all these balloons? Do you have more somewhere?" I lifted up his shirt to check underneath. "You're not ticklish are you?"

Carter's eyes went wide and he shook his head. All it took was one finger on his side and an unmanly giggle popped out. He grabbed my hands and sat up, pulling me onto his lap.

"Think you're so tough, little lady? I think I missed a spot." Tyson tossed him another balloon and Carter squeezed it over my head. I wiped the water out of my eyes and he pushed the stringy bits of hair out of my face. I probably looked awful but he grinned at me, guessing my thoughts. "You've never looked better."

The look he was giving me as he leaned in was almost like he was about to... I arched my back as a hard slap hit me like, well, like an angry water balloon in the back. I turned around to see Holly baring down on us, armed with another water balloon. She grinned, like it was all in fun, but the wild look in her eyes told me otherwise.

I tumbled off Carter's lap and stood up, brushing the wet grass off my bum and trying to pull the now sopping wet bathrobe around me. Carter stood up, as well, laughingly grabbing up a few more water balloons from a bucket, but he stepped in front of me, blocking me from Holly. He chased her across the yard and she giggled in delight, knowing that for the moment she'd won.

***

I didn't see Carter again until our piano lesson the next day, but he was aloof, like he couldn't wait to get away from me. I tried to ignore the fact that he went out of his way to not touch me, moving away if his arm or leg brushed against mine, and focused on my playing. It was better not to think, not to feel, for the moment. During our last lesson, Carter had told me to avoid memorizing the songs, and instead to go slow and force myself to read the notes. I'd taken his handwritten staff and gone over it in my spare time, which I had a lot of. He begrudgingly admired how much progress I'd made, but when I turned and smiled at him he looked away, almost like it pained him.

Dave didn't lecture Carter this time. He'd decided our lessons would be heavily edited with music and close ups anyway. He stepped out for a phone call for most of it. At the end though, he wanted me to look up from my playing and stare dreamily into Carter's eyes. I had to do it seven times before Dave was satisfied. Carter stared back at me with an intensity that was almost worse than the disinterest he'd shown minutes before. Why was he doing this to me?

When Dave waved us off at the end of our lesson, I followed a few steps behind Carter to his apartment door, and dashed in at the last minute, cutting off the cameraman walking behind me and locking the door.

"Bethany, what are you doing in here?"

Carter glanced around and I followed his lead, checking the apartment for Tyson or Weston, but we were alone.

Suddenly, I didn't know what I was doing. I'd been so mad and wanted an explanation. But now I was mostly nervous, and a little embarrassed.

Carter studied me for a minute and then walked over and touched my cheek. "I know I'm confusing you," he whispered. "I'm sorry."

He wrapped his hands around my waist and picked me up, carrying me back toward the front door. Was he throwing me out of his apartment? He put me down and reached around for the door knob, but didn't open the door. Instead, he sighed and dropped his head into my neck. His hands were still gripping my waist.

"You have to go," he murmured, even as his lips puckered in the spot where my neck and shoulders meet. I turned my face towards him, my cheek brushing against his. He lifted his head and looked at me, his eyes reflecting a kaleidoscope of conflicting emotions. I moved first, standing on tiptoe to reach his lips. The kiss went from hesitant to demanding in an instant, for both of us. But after what seemed like only seconds, he unwound his arms from around me and stepped back, shaking his head, like he was trying to clear it. He wouldn't meet my eyes again. "You should go."

So I did, thoroughly confused, irritated, and covered in goosebumps from his touch. I stood outside his door, trying to get my bearings, trying to breathe again. Trying not to bang on the door and make him kiss me like that again.

Finally, I turned and walked back to my apartment, my body still a shaky, tingly mess. I didn't say a word about it to Michelle, even when she teased me about my piano lesson. I couldn't even look at her, afraid she would see the inner torment Carter was causing me and ask about it. As little as I understood him before, I really didn't understand him now.

CHAPTER 13

With a few hours to kill before elimination night, I ran to the Jacuzzi as soon as Jada and Marco were finished with it. They were such hot tub hogs.

I had just closed my eyes and felt my stress melting, when a disturbance in the water let me know Dave sent someone over for me. He had this dumb rule about needing a partner in the hot tub for our "safety," when we all knew what he truly wanted was a romance-only hot tub. I wasn't the only one trying to sneak in here on my own. A few days ago I'd seen Holly get in by herself before Dave forced Max to join her. I was actually looking forward to seeing that footage.

I kept my eyes closed, hoping maybe if I didn't see who it was they wouldn't try to talk to me. A hand touched my thigh, and I instinctively whacked whoever it was in the face with the back of my hand.

"Ouch. Dang it, Bethany. I was only teasing."

Weston. Why did it have to be him? I opened my eyes and glared at him. "What happened to your crush on me? You toss me aside for my roommate?"

Weston laughed before going to fake contrition. "I'm confused, baby. Michelle is a beautiful woman and I want to keep my options open." He scooted closer and put his arm around me. I was about to pull away, but then he leaned into my ear and whispered, "I know you think we had a thing, but I need you to promise you won't vote for me tonight. I have to get off this show."

Ignoring the whole, 'we had a thing' comment, I asked, "Why not leave now?"

"Forfeit the money and pay my way home? No way."

"I thought a hotshot lawyer like you didn't worry about money," I whispered back.

"Look, my dad was going to help me out with law school, but he's got four ex-wives breathing down his neck and three kids under the age of five, and he'll be seventy next year. Which means my student loan and credit card debts are all mine. Plus, I have a balloon payment coming up on a house I shouldn't have bought. Someday I'm going to have loads of money and no one hanging on me to take their piece of it, but right now I need quick cash, so yes, I'm staying until I'm voted off. But the longer I'm here the less likely my law firm is going to be patient with the sob story I gave them about my true love coming on this show without me. Especially since I just voted her off."

Wow, this explained so many things about Weston.

"I'm not into revenge," I told him. "You have nothing to fear from me, but you may need to talk to Michelle." I almost regretted telling him, but I was pretty sure Michelle was going to vote for Weston if she could find another way to keep Patrick on the show without having to vote for him herself.

***

At the cocktail party before elimination, Holly cornered me. Dave and crew followed, so my hackles were already raised.

"You can't have Carter, you know," she said. "He's not here for love. He just wants to be famous."

"Okay."

Her eyes narrowed. She wouldn't be put off so easily. "I've known him forever. He probably knows me better than I know myself. But I don't think I know him. Does that make sense?"

I didn't answer right away, letting my mind try to unravel that puzzle. "No, it doesn't."

"He lets you think you're close to him, but he won't let anyone in, not even me."

"Then why haven't you given up?" I asked.

She smiled bitterly and shrugged. "That's the problem. He gives you just enough that you hold onto that hope, thinking maybe someday he'll feel the way about you that you do about him. But it's an illusion."

I knew she was playing mind games with me, but there had to be a sprinkling of truth somewhere, too. Wasn't there? She was impossible to figure out. Carter had been forthright about everything so far, except her. If she wasn't eliminated tonight, I would make him fess up.

She was still staring at me.

"Well thanks for telling me," I offered, hoping she'd walk off. I had my own issues with Carter, I didn't need to hear about hers.

"Has he kissed you yet?"

Be casual. I shrugged. "Yeah, I guess." *It was awesome. It's all I can think about. Don't picture it. Don't.*

Holly watched my face and the truth must have leaked out of it. She gave me a disgusted look and threw her hands in the air before stalking off to attach herself to Carter's side. He glanced at me questioningly, but Greg tinged his glass and we all turned our attention to him.

***

As we were filing into the conference room, I took the opportunity to nudge Michelle. "What'd you decide to do? With your vote?"

She winked at me. "You'll see. It's all good."

The conference room was decorated like a children's classroom. That was the instant vibe I got. Colorful drawings and posters lined the walls, and a long art table with tiny chairs sat in the middle. It was assigned seating again, but instead of neat little place cards, they had laminated name plates taped to the table with our names written in crayon. Like this was our classroom. And we were adult children. The irony was not lost on me.

I sat down and adjusted my striped slacks. Not pinstripes, but thick bands of yellow and black. I chose them because they fit well, their one redeeming quality. Tyson had already complimented me on them, saying I looked like a hot bumblebee.

Greg cleared his throat and began his speech. He was wearing spectacles and a bow tie and he tried to sound teacher-like as he asked us if we'd learned anything this week. We all nodded like good students and endured the rest of his speech, filled with other obvious preschool references. This was not as exciting now that I'd been through the first elimination night. I tried to avoid glancing at Carter. When I did, I only got distracted by thoughts of his face in my neck and our amazing kiss, before he pushed me away. What did it all mean?

An assistant handed out blank papers and crayons while Greg explained that we were to write down our vote and then flip the paper over until it was our turn.

The voting began with Jada and Marco, obvious choices there, and Sylvie and Eddie, obvious choices there as well. Sylvie drew Eddie's name with swirly letters surrounded by hearts. He dotted the eye in Sylvie with a flower. It was adorable and we ooohed and ahhhed appropriately.

Clearly, Dave was trying to save the uncertain votes for last.

Carter held up his paper. HOLLY. He'd drawn a picture of a holly leaf with berries. She blushed and held up her paper. CARTER xoxoxo smiley face. Carter smiled back, but it looked kind of wooden. Maybe it was only my wishful thinking. Why did he keep voting for her if he didn't like her?

We turned our attention to Tyson. He'd written an acrostic poem with my name. Oh my gosh, how embarrassing.

B is for Beautiful
E is for Extra tempting
T is for Terrific
H is for HOT!
A is for All of it, the total package
N is for Nice
Y is for You know it!

I'm sure I resembled a tomato, but I took the paper from Tyson and smoothed it out. I'd be showing this to my canasta partners at the rest home someday...while we laughed hysterically.

I looked up and caught Carter's eyes flashing from me to Tyson and then back to me. His expression was like someone left out of a private joke. Jealousy. I couldn't deny it anymore. Some girls might use that to their advantage. Dave would surely want me to. But I didn't want Carter to pursue me because he thought someone else was. I pushed away the dreary thought that Carter might have only kissed me because Tyson did. It was too depressing.

My turn. Focusing back on the task at hand, I held up my

paper with Tyson's name neatly printed. I felt a little like the nerd at the cool kids table with my plain paper. No drawings of hearts or flowers or anything on mine.

Tyson seemed pleased anyway and I grinned back at him.

Michelle's turn was next and I was surprised when she looked right at Patrick and held up her paper. PATRICK, *are we ever going to talk?*

Patrick gave her an embarrassed smile and then held up his paper. HOLLY. He'd drawn kissy lips after it. Michelle's face dropped. She put her paper down and started fiddling with it. Her acting had gotten better. If I didn't know her better, I would have fallen for it.

Holly snorted at him dismissively and then all eyes turned to Weston. He was grinning like a kid at Christmas, knowing he was being sent home, but quickly reigned himself in and put on a solemn face.

He shook his head as he lifted up his paper. MICHELLE, written out in pink crayon. "I'm sorry the feelings weren't mutual," he told her. "I was hoping for some time in the hot tub with you before I left."

Michelle rolled her eyes, reaching over and tousling his hair. "In your dreams, buddy."

After saying goodbye to Weston, we all sat back down while Greg served up peanut butter and jelly sandwiches cut into cute triangles with small glasses of milk. Carter leaned across the table and held his glass out. My face flushed as I clinked mine against his. And then I looked away, not wanting him to see how flustered he could make me with one glance.

CHAPTER 14

"What are you doing?"

Carter whirled around. "Oh, you scared me." He turned off the lawnmower and rested his arm across it. It was the morning after elimination night and the sound of the mower made me curious enough to change my route and find *this*. Carter, shirtless, bronze and lean in the sun. No big deal. Just because he looked like he should be on the cover of a romance novel...not that I read those.

"I couldn't take any more sitting around. I found a shed with landscaping tools and decided to mow the lawn. I needed to clear my head, have something to do. Dave liked the idea so much he had Greg tells us we have to do this as part of our chores. They made me take my shirt off. I thought you were Greg coming back with sun tan oil or something." He shuddered and I laughed. He looked horrified at the thought.

Tyson came around the corner. Somehow, he'd gotten a hold of another pair of hideous jean cut-offs, even shorter than the first pair. That and a pair of Converse high tops were all he wore, a set of long pruning shears draped casually over one shoulder. He winked at me and then continued strutting over to the boxwood bushes. They were in desperate need of a trim.

My plan to take a nap by the pool again seemed extremely lazy in the face of their industry.

"Can I help?"

Carter gave me a lopsided smile. "Of course. But, be careful or they'll put us all in some horrible calendar. Another moneymaking scheme by Dave Maxwell."

I laughed. "Can't you picture it? The Landscape Calendar, with Carter as Mr. March, posing in the green grass. And Tyson, Mr. December. We'll find him a scarf to go with those horrible shorts he's wearing. What month would I be?"

"If it was my calendar you'd be on every month." Carter turned a little bit red, as if he didn't mean to be quite so flirtatious and bent down to check the grass bag. "If you want to help, there's a rake and a broom in the shed back there. Take your pick."

I skipped over to the shed and got out the broom, my heart doing little flip-flops. Maybe it was only a line, but it still warmed me to hear it.

The lawnmower had blown a fine layer of grass dust all over the sidewalks and I took my time sweeping it back onto the lawn. Only occasionally did I let my eyes wander. Okay, maybe more than occasionally. Carter caught me once and grinned, making me drop my head and sweep even more furiously.

When Tyson finished trimming the bushes, he recruited me to help him rake up the cut branches into piles and stuff them into garbage bags. For the first time in days, I felt useful and busy, like I was accomplishing something. The cameras didn't even bother me as much. I found out that Tyson was the baby of his family with six older sisters. All of them were married and they constantly tried to set him up on blind dates.

"Was Gretchen a blind date?" I asked.

Tyson wrinkled his nose. "Um no. She's a friend of my sister, Christina, but Christina's exact words were 'do not date her' so of course then I had to." He laughed. "We lasted six weeks, mostly because it was too much fun to see Christina fuming mad at me."

"Why didn't she want you to date Gretchen?"

"Gretchen tells her friends everything about her relationships. Every obnoxious detail. Imagine my sister with her hands over her ears for six weeks."

"That's horrible." I tried to keep a straight face, but a snort escaped. Tyson's eyes went wide and we both burst into a fit of laughter.

Tyson stretched his arms above his head, groaning a little bit. "We should go for a swim."

"Sounds good," Carter said from behind me, before draping his arm around my shoulder. Carter, acting possessive? This was new.

Tyson raised an eyebrow at him, but didn't retract his invitation.

Glancing down at Tyson's cut-offs, I smirked. "You'll have to go put on swim trunks first. Those things will probably get water logged and fall off."

Tyson grinned. "And that would be a problem?"

He avoided my swatting hands and jogged upstairs to change, calling behind him, "Carter's in jeans, too."

Too late, I realized when I'd chased Tyson off, it made Carter drop his arm from around my shoulder. I hope he didn't think I did it on purpose.

"Do you mind if I come? I wouldn't want to interrupt your time with Tyson."

I turned to face Carter. "Of course I want you to come. You're probably all hot and itchy from the grass." I blushed as he looked down at his chest. There were bits of grass clinging to him all over. He reached out and brushed a little piece off my shoulder where it'd gotten stuck to my tank top.

"Sorry, I didn't mean to get grass all over you." He took a step closer and carefully drew another piece of grass out of a strand of my hair, taking his time. My stomach fluttered and I took in a shaky breath, willing my hands to stay at my side and not try to clean the grass off him.

"I don't mind," I said, looking up into his face. He didn't seem to know what to do with his hands, now that I was grass free. He dropped them to his sides, but then inched them out to brush against my hands before interlocking his fingers with mine.

He stared down at our hands, not saying anything. A minute went by with us like that, nothing happening except for Carter's thumbs rubbing across the backs of my hands. I leaned in and tucked my head under his chin, enjoying the sun on my back, the feel of his warm skin against my cheek, the way his deep breaths released puffs of air across the top of my head, and the funny surety that I was now completely covered in grass.

"Hey," Tyson called from behind us. "Can't leave you two alone for five minutes. I saw a pool volleyball net when I was putting away the tools. Come help me get it out of the shed."

Carter and I broke apart, grinning at each other sheepishly. We walked over to the shed and the guys each took a weighted pole, rolling them over to a side of the pool while I carried the net. Leaving my tank top and gym shorts on a deck chair, I jumped in the pool and helped Tyson set up the net while Carter ran upstairs to change.

We got a game of volleyball going, although I wasn't much help to Tyson's team. Carter was like a machine, slamming down the ball on our side no matter what we did. After losing miserably, we started lightly volleying the ball back and forth, giving me a chance to hit it without worrying it might come back and spike me in the nose.

"Is it weird, you two, being roommates?" I asked.

"Yes," they both answered.

"I mean, Weston was a bathroom hog. He'd shower for forty-five minutes. But at least he wore pants."

Tyson scoffed. "It's not like I walk around naked. I would at home, but I keep the skivvies on around here, right?"

"He wears briefs. Walking around in boxers I could handle."

"I don't see the difference. Just because I like to keep everything tucked in tight."

"Stop, stop." I splashed Tyson. "You're being gross."

"He brought it up," Tyson said, giving us his most innocent face. "But I bet that wasn't what Bethany was asking about, was it Bethy? When she asked if things were weird."

"Not really interested in what type of underwear y'all wear, but thanks for the info. And don't call me Bethy."

"Sure thing, Betharina." Tyson ducked under the water to avoid the tidal wave of water I splashed his way and swam towards me, his hands reaching out for my legs under the water. I screamed when he caught me, as my body lifted up and catapulted through the air, landing with a big splash. But I'd managed to take a breath and close my mouth before impact, so at least I wasn't coughing when I came up.

"What were you saying?" I asked Tyson, wiping the water off my face. "What did you think I was asking?"

Tyson grinned while Carter shot him a warning look. "Hey, I never promised to keep quiet about anything. It's a free country."

What the heck? I glanced back and forth between the two of them, trying to figure out what was going on.

"Bethany wants to know if it's weird that we're rooming together while we're both after her hot body. Am I right, Bethalicious?"

"Fine, you can call me Bethy," I stammered, so ready to change the subject. He was right, dang him. That was what I'd meant. It didn't mean he had to spell it out for all of us.

But Tyson went right on. "Carter grills me, before every elimination night. 'You're voting for Bethany, right?' Like he gets two votes or something."

I turned to look at Carter for confirmation and he rubbed his forehead, his eyes wide. "Thank you, Tyson."

Tyson took a bow. "Honesty is the best policy. That's what my gram taught me." He picked up the forgotten ball and lobbed it over the net to Carter. We went back to volleying in awkward silence until Hurricane Holly came bearing down on us, doing that jerky knee walk thing she did when she was upset.

"Your delightful ex is on her way over here," Tyson said, trying not to laugh. "She looks super happy."

Dang it, I had been enjoying a Holly-free morning.

"Carter," she said, sharply. "Carter, I have the date night card. We have a date tonight."

"Oh. Sounds good," he answered, pasting a stiff smile on his face. We were all waiting for the bad news she seemed to be carrying around with her like a rain cloud.

"With them. It's a double date. With those two." She wrinkled her nose as she pointed in our direction. "We're country line dancing."

Carter moaned at the same time that Tyson let out a whoop.

CHAPTER 15

As the loud intro to "Achy Breaky Heart" pumped out of the speakers, Carter glanced over at me and let out a deep sigh. "I hate this song so much I want to murder it."

Perhaps Dave was mining our conversations for material. Poor Carter had admitted on camera he couldn't dance.

"Yes, Billy Ray Cyrus has launched several great gifts into our culture, hasn't he?" Carter cracked a smile, but then it dropped back into a face of pure dread. I tried again. "This is like, the easiest line dance on the face of the earth. Trust me. All you have to do is walk up and down and clap when everyone else does."

Tyson and Holly were already demonstrating the dance with flair while we waited for the instructor to finish getting a microphone pinned to her shirt. They grinned at each other as they moved in perfect unison. So Holly actually liked something. Maybe she was human after all.

"I thought Holly was mad we were line dancing."

Carter looked over at Fred Astaire and Ginger and sighed. "She knows better than to take me dancing. She's even called me a killjoy on several occasions. I think mostly she doesn't like that you're here."

There was no way Holly heard us over the music, but she picked that exact moment to turn and sneer at me. If she was upset I was hanging out with her date, she could triple step her way over here and help him out. He looked like he was about to lose his breakfast.

The music stopped and the instructor clapped her hands and motioned for us to line up, before starting the track again.

"Everybody ready?" She didn't wait for an answer. "And one, two, three, four, heel tap, heel tap, toe tap, toe tap, kick, rock back. Clap, shimmy, cross over, stomp, stomp, scuff forward."

I momentarily forgot about Carter as I tried to keep up. This was not the dance I remembered. And there was no herd to follow, no one to hide behind and copy. I looked up to see Dave laughing at us, doubled over. Assistants next to him were covering their mouths and pointing at...I turned and took in Carter's dancing. Oh, I so wanted to kick Dave where it counted. Carter's arms were flopping like a marionette as he desperately tried to kick and stomp at the right times. Which was not happening. A sheen of sweat beaded on his forehead.

In his defense, he looked amazing in Wranglers and boots. But I wasn't digging on the leather fringe hanging off his western shirt. It only drew more attention to the arm flopping. He turned and caught me staring.

"You don't have to say it. I know what I look like," he huffed out as we attempted our slide, turn, clap. "I'm reconsidering my first plan, which was to hide in the bathroom and refuse to come out."

"Sorry. Holly's already done that."

"What?" Carter missed the cue to slide left and bumped into me. He put his hand out to steady me and I linked arms with him so I could help him out with his steps and we could talk. We glanced over at Holly, but she hadn't heard us.

"The first day, when we were reading about our exes being on the show, Holly ran into that bathroom over there and locked herself in. She refused to come out and yelled mean things through the door at Greg."

"What is she...? Why is she....?" Carter eyebrows scrunched in concentration and he didn't finish his thought.

If he didn't understand it, how was I supposed to?

The music ended and we collapsed into chairs while assistants brought us water bottles. Holly turned to Carter and smirked. "That was some fine dancing there, partner." She reached out and smoothed his collar, before stealing the cowboy hat atop his head and plopping it on hers. "How do I look?"

Her flirting was so obnoxious. I stood up and walked over to examine the ugly decorations set up as a backdrop to our dance space. Atop the hay bales sat a fake rooster with beady eyes, a tin washtub filled with sunflowers (also fake), and a set of old cowboy boots with a hat propped over them.

Sharp clapping brought me around. We weren't done. "Any Man of Mine," by Shania Twain, blasted out of the speakers and I reluctantly walked over to stand in our line again. There was no way Carter would be able to keep up with this one. I caught his eye and mouthed, "You okay?"

He nodded. "I like this song."

Well, he wouldn't like it in a minute. After we got past the stomp, stomp, claps, the real work began. The instructor started calling out a blur of right together, left together, step, hip, hip, turn, cha-cha. Her feet were doing things I knew mine would never be capable of, no matter how many times we repeated it.

Carter touched my arm and showed off his modified version, which consisted of marching in place until it was time to turn. I grinned and joined him. Better than floundering after everyone else. We started adding in ridiculous, but easy flairs, like jazz hands and shoulder shrugs, laughing at each other's super uncool moves. He turned and pretended to lasso me and it suddenly occurred to me, this wasn't dance jail. We could dance however we wanted. I gave him a saucy look and started jumping toward him to the beat of the music, until his 'lasso' wrangled me in. He took my arms and placed them up around his neck, grinning down at me as we swayed side-to-side.

"Having fun yet?" I asked.

"Now I am."

Holly saw us and grabbed Tyson, forcing him into an impressive Texas Two Step. We stopped dancing and clapped along as Tyson twirled, lifted and tossed Holly before bending her in a low dip to finish the song. They were amazing together. Another song started up and it didn't take much encouragement to get them to do it again.

Carter leaned over and whispered in my ear. "Do you think they would notice if we ducked out of here?" His hand curled around mine and I took in a long shaky breath. Yes, I wanted to be anywhere with him, go anywhere he wanted to go, but that very feeling was why I also needed to hold back. Hormones were messing with my ability to reason or wonder why sometimes he was hot and sometimes he was cold.

"Technically, I'm supposed to be Tyson's date and you're supposed to be Holly's."

"They'll get over it."

Tyson might, but I knew Holly wouldn't. Sometimes Carter catered to her every whim, but he didn't seem all that concerned with her feelings at the moment. It was time. It was time for him to lay it all out and tell me what the heck was going on.

"Okay, watch me. Wait a minute, and then follow." I casually edged over to the decorations again, pretending to study them. There was a door right behind there and I backed up until I was leaning against it. After checking camera angles and faces, I ducked out and hid behind a pillar, waiting for Carter to join me.

He came through the door a minute after me and we ran together, toward the apartments. A cameraman with his back to us was filming Michelle reading by the pool. If she saw us, she did a good job pretending not to. We ran up the stairs and stopped to catch our breaths behind another pillar.

"Come with me." I grabbed his hand and dragged him down the hall. He laced his fingers through mine and I ignored the jolt of happiness that gesture brought me as I pulled him into my apartment and shut the door. Carter let go of my hand and turned my shoulders towards him. His face was full of questions, but also a little bit of anticipation.

I was about to be a total buzz-kill, but I wanted answers.

"Carter, I want to know about Holly, away from the cameras."

He dropped his hands and the smile left his eyes. I caught an almost imperceptible shake of his head before he turned and dropped onto my couch, knitting his hands behind his head.

"What about Holly?"

What about Holly? He asks as if I'm the crazy one. I pushed back my irritation and sat down on the other end of the couch, pulling off my ridiculous cowgirl boots and adjusting my jean cut-offs. At least mine were a little more modest than the Tyson variety, hitting mid-thigh. And they had the cutest bandana-patterned, star-shaped patches over the pockets. These I might take with me after the show.

Carter still wasn't saying anything. I tucked my legs up so I could rest my chin on them and turned to look at Carter. I'd just wait him out. There was no way he was putting this off any longer.

Carter stared back at me and I could see the stubbornness setting in. This was the most annoying staring contest ever, but I was going to win. And I was going to enjoy the view. His dark grey-blue eyes were beautiful, even though they made me so mad right now. And he had great eyebrows, slightly darker in color than the rest of his hair. Not something I'd noticed before. I started studying his face, piece by piece, memorizing the planes of his nose and following his jaw-line until I knew I could draw it without looking at him. He seemed to be watching me the same way, but I didn't let my mind dwell on that too much. Until he started edging towards me.

"What are you doing?" I asked as his face drew closer to mine and his arm came to rest on top of the couch behind my head. He was still studying me, and I bit my lip. "You're making me nervous."

"Oh, I am?" He sat back, but not before gently pulling my legs out and stretching them across the couch so my calves were over his lap. "Bethany, what am I going to do about you? I promised I wouldn't tell anyone, but you seem to reach around all my defenses like this super attractive cyborg."

"Did you just call me a cyborg?"

"A super attractive one. Quit distracting me with your words and your legs." He slid his hand around my calf and sighed. "Did I tell you I'm a legs man? I didn't know until recently."

What was he talking about? My confusion must have shown in my face because he laughed. "I know, what does this have to do with Holly? I didn't think I'd get close enough to anyone that I'd need to explain."

"Well you need to explain." He was the one being distracting. I wanted to make him stay on topic, but I'd never had anyone play with my legs before. He was running his fingers along my shins, tracing spirals in them. It was taking all my concentration to remember why we were sitting there.

Carter took a deep breath. "Holly's an old friend. She was all set to come on the show. Didn't know about the ex-boyfriend twist. Clueless, like the rest of you. But then her ex got a DUI and the show had to scramble. They called her up, explained the situation and offered to keep her if she could come up with another ex." He smiled sheepishly. "Me."

Clueless, like the rest of you.

"We've never dated. I'm not sure why she decided to go with the whole crazy jealousy bit. If I ask her about it she says I'm spending too much time with you, that I'm not keeping my promise. You see, I agreed to help her stay as long as possible and play the part of her ex. Act like we might want to get back together. She's hoping this will launch her acting career."

I thought back to Holly locking herself in the bathroom and dragging Carter off the picnic bench. It was all an act. Every bit of it. He played the part and I was dumb enough to fall for it. I yanked my legs back and stood up, needing some space from him.

"You said you came on here for your sister. Do you even have a sister?" It came out more hysterical than I wanted it to.

"Calm down and let me explain."

Calm down was something Todd used to say if I ever tried to stand up for myself. Todd always acted like I was hyper-sensitive, to the point where I was the one apologizing when he'd insulted me. I did not want to calm down.

"Get out."

His face registered shock. "I have a sister, Bethany."

"Out."

CHAPTER 16

Carter either returned to the dance date or got dragged there, because when an irate Dave and cameras pounded on my apartment door and insisted I come back with them, Carter was already back at the conference room, doing a half-hearted shuffle to another country song.

I lined up next to him, but refused to turn my head, throwing all my concentration on the directions the instructor called out. My mind churned with all the possible editing things Dave could do with this date. The tension oozing between us was thick enough to spread on a cracker.

"Beth, I'm sorry."

"Don't call me Beth."

"Sorry."

"Pay attention to your date, like you're supposed to. Dave is already mad at us for taking off."

Carter shook his head. "He's only upset he didn't catch us together. I bet when you answered your apartment door alone, it just made it look like you needed a snack break or something."

"Ha. Ha." I wouldn't fall victim to his charm again. The anger coursing through me felt empowering. Even my dancing was better. How did I ever think love and reality TV could co-exist? No one else did.

My legs kicked and stomped for the last time as the song ended, much to my relief. I ignored Carter and grabbed Tyson's arm, smiling up at him. He leaned over, resting his head near my ear.

"You okay? You look like you're trying to smile while passing a gallstone."

I laughed, but tears were threatening. *Don't lose it now.* Empowering was unraveling into embarrassing. "Ah, Tyson. You really know how to flatter a lady."

He must have realized how not okay I was. He threw an arm around me and led us out of the conference room, calling over his shoulder, "You might want to follow us, because I'm going to go kiss Bethany goodnight, and it will be epic."

"Now, wait, wait a minute." Greg ran after us, a stream of new directions spewing out of his mouth. "We still have a candle-lit dinner for you. So yes, take fifteen minutes and go change. But save the epic goodnight kiss for later." He motioned a cameraman over and the guy walked backwards the whole way upstairs, catching our faces as we headed back to the apartments. They must practice that at film school. I'd fall and break something.

Tyson squeezed my hand and left me at the door of my apartment. Opening and slamming it behind me never felt so good.

I took one look at Michelle and the waterworks burst forth.

Michelle twisted her hands together. "Oh dear, I'm not good with crying. What happened? Was the dancing that bad?"

I shook my head. Even if I had any words, my body was incapable of letting them out. I'd only known Carter a week, seven days. Not enough time to fall in love. Nothing made sense anymore. At this point, I'd pay money to understand why I was crying.

Standing in front of the closet racks didn't help my emotional state. I didn't want to take off the first cute thing I'd worn on this show. Mechanically, I undressed, dropping my country dancewear in the hamper and putting on a sundress that would've been okay if it didn't look like the big red flowers on it were hemorrhaging.

Michelle helped me fix my makeup. We couldn't talk. My thoughts were still too tangled and I could tell she had no idea what to say. So she made it up to me the only way she knew how. Even with the lingering red blotches on my cheeks, her makeup skills were far superior to mine. Feeling a bit more confident, I left the apartment to go meet Tyson.

He stood up and pulled out my chair for me as I approached our small table, the sun setting as a backdrop. It was a little windy and the candles in the middle went out repeatedly, sending an assistant scurrying over to relight them again and again.

A waitress approached to bring us our dinner salads. We recognized her as the hair/makeup girl and exchanged looks. I almost choked on my mouthful of salad when Greg glided around the table, grinning like a lunatic as he serenaded us on the violin. He was dressed all in black, with a beret hanging off his head.

"When is the balloon animal guy coming?" Tyson whispered, giving me a wink.

"I learned how to make those. My brother and I ran a booth at a school fair in middle school."

"Cool. What animals can you make?"

I kept the chit-chat up and tried to smile at the right times, but it felt mechanical and Tyson clearly sensed it.

He dropped his fork. "All right. Spill it, sister. I'm putting my friend hat on. I'll pull it off later tonight, when I take advantage of your fight with Carter and kiss you until you don't remember him."

"What makes you say we had a fight?"

Tyson squeezed the bridge of his nose and frowned at me. "Everything."

I couldn't tell Tyson the truth. Not on camera. Dave wouldn't want me to reveal to all of America that Carter was a substitute ex. A fluke. We'd all laughed about Weston being an actor, when it was Carter all along.

"He lied to me."

"About what?" Tyson smirked. "Let me guess. He lied about Holly."

My mouth dropped open and I quickly closed it. "Then you know?"

Tyson leaned back in his chair and peered at me thoughtfully. "No. I have no idea what's going on between Carter and Holly. My theory? She saved him from a terrible industrial accident and now requires his everlasting servitude. Because that's the chemistry I'm getting from him. Obligation. His chemistry towards you is more like a repressed aching need for your bod."

Talking about this on camera was giving me an aching need to change the subject. "So Holly's a good dancer."

"Yep. She is. She pretends to hate me, but no one dances with Tyson and leaves untouched."

"I bet." I covered my mouth to keep the snort of laughter inside. Tyson's eyes sparkled mischievously and I lifted my glass. "You're too much. But thank you for helping me feel better. Sorry I've been such a lousy date."

After dinner, Tyson walked me to my door, where he gave me a big hug and a small kiss. Despite all his talk, he was the most warm-hearted and intuitive guy friend I'd ever had.

***

My goal the next day: avoid Carter. If I could get to another elimination night and off this atrocious show, maybe my life could get back to normal. Normal was sounding less and less dreary.

Dave quickly smashed those plans by dropping in after breakfast and letting me know a piano lesson with Carter would start in fifteen minutes.

Fabulous.

Twenty minutes later, I sat down next to Carter in the conference room and took a deep breath. *Professional. Act professional.* Carter touched my elbow and my fingers clanged down on the keys.

"Bethany, I—"

"All right, you love birds," Greg interrupted, rubbing his hands together. "Would it be possible for the two of you to play a duet? Dave thinks it would be romantic."

"Right now?" I asked.

Greg and Carter both turned to look at me, but I stared down at my hands. They were pulsing hot and cold in turns. Maybe I was coming down with something.

"Well, it would help if we had books." Carter threw an irritated look at Dave. "But I could write something out for Bethany and improvise my part, I guess."

He grabbed his notebook and started scribbling music notes on it, occasionally checking it against the piano. After a few minutes he placed the notebook in front of me and showed me my hand position. Three notes into it, an immovable lump rose in my throat. "Canon in D", by Pachelbel. I'd known since the sixth grade, when boys stopped being icky, that someday I'd walk down the aisle to it. It didn't matter if it was overused or overplayed. To me it was the most beautiful song in the world.

Carter leaned over and his thigh brushed against mine. "You're doing great."

Now my legs were tingling. It was awfully cruel that attraction and logic did not exist in the same sphere. My body didn't seem to care if I was mad at him. I told myself it didn't mean anything. Of course he would pick this song. Except for the notes being farther apart than I'd tried before, it was a simple part, slow and steady, perfect for a beginner student. After the third run through, I was ready for him to join me.

For two lines he simply added the left hand, creating chords to go with my simple part. Then he reached around me for the high notes, his chin tickling my hair and his chest expanding with every breath against my back. If I slowed a little, or hesitated before hitting a note, he'd pause with me, as if we'd intended it that way. Dang it, Dave was right. The synergy between us was…romantic.

"Last time through," Carter whispered. We let out twin breaths of air as the last notes hovered.

I almost expected clapping or oohs and ahhs, but I looked up and took in the ugly conference room, camera lenses, people moving back and forth, Dave yawning. This wasn't a Jane Austen novel. This was TV.

Suddenly, I didn't want Carter's praise, excuses, or explanations. And I definitely didn't want the electricity that coursed through me from just a whisper of his touch. The need to get away was overwhelming, but I'd stormed off too many times on this show already. Oh, the craziness of it all. I'd used up all my dramatic exits in the first week. Well, maybe I could have one more. I wouldn't be staying much longer.

"This was fun. Thanks." I plastered a smile on my face, patted Carter's back, and swung my legs around. He looked confused, but I bolted from the room and didn't stop until I reached my apartment.

An unhappy Dave stopped by, as I expected. Michelle told him I felt sick and needed sleep. Carter came a few minutes later and she gave him the same excuse. It bought me a few hours. Fidgety hours. If nothing else, we were well rested on this show. The last thing I needed was another nap. TV annoyed me. I couldn't concentrate on my book. Nothing sounded good to eat. Michelle left me to go off somewhere with Patrick. I didn't know where their hiding place was and I never asked. Plausible deniability and all that.

After checking the hallway, I finally made a run for the gym. I'd never tried to jog off restless energy before, but it sounded like a good idea.

A half mile into my run on the treadmill, the endorphins hit and I grinned. This wasn't a good idea, this was a great idea. I added incline and speed. If I couldn't run off this show, I could at least picture myself sprinting out of here. Climbing over mountains to blow this pop stand.

At first I'd watched the glass door religiously, afraid of being caught faking sick. But I got lost in my mountain climbing fantasy, deep into my second mile, puffing out the words to "Climb Every Mountain." So it startled me to see Carter watching me from the doorway, hiding a smile behind his hand.

My foot came down between the track and the edging, throwing my balance. A sense of doom and embarrassment jolted through me as my legs buckled and my bottom hit the end of the treadmill before sliding into the wall.

Carter rushed over, smacking the power button as he dropped in front of me. He put his hands gently on each side of my face.

"Bethany, you okay? Don't move yet. I'm so sorry I spooked you. This is all my fault." His face crinkled with worry.

"I'm fine." I made the mistake of wincing.

"I should go for help so you can get checked out."

"No!" I grabbed the front of his shirt. "No cameras. Please."

"Are you dizzy? Any pain, tingling or numbness in your back or neck?"

"My shoulder blade hurts a little where it hit the wall. But look…" I moved my neck and lifted a leg. "I think I'm ready to get off the floor." I started to stand up and he put his arms under me.

"Go slow. Hold on to the bar of the treadmill."

"Such a worrier. I'm fine." And amazingly, I was. I didn't even land on my tailbone. One side of my rear end would soon bruise beautifully, but all in all, I was okay.

Carter led me out of the gym and fussed over me the entire way upstairs. We passed Sylvie and Eddie heading down to the pool, but they were too involved in each other to even notice us.

Once Carter had me settled on my couch, he ran out to the ice machine and came back with two bags of ice wrapped in towels and a packet of ibuprofen. He sat down next to me while I awkwardly positioned one icepack under me and one behind my back.

"I'm still mad at you. You kicked me out of your apartment once. I should make you leave mine."

Carter stared into my eyes. "Can I explain now? Please? Besides, you might have a concussion. I should stay and monitor you for a while."

"Are you a doctor?"

He cocked his head like a disapproving parent. "After dealing with people all day who don't have a clue what to do after calling 911, my dad became a little obsessed with preparing us for emergencies. Would you like to see my CPR certification?"

"No."

"Can I stay?"

Dang it. Now I wasn't sure. He took my hesitation as a yes and grinned.

"You lied to me."

"I didn't tell you the whole truth at first."

"That's still lying. But I get it. You had to protect the show. Protect Holly."

Carter touched my hand. "I was an idiot. I didn't know how to tell you, and I made it sound like this was some lark Holly and I cooked up. No, I never would have come on a dating show if she hadn't asked me. I didn't want to. But I made the mistake of talking to my little sister about it. And she immediately latched onto the idea. I promise everything I told you about her is true."

"It's okay, Carter. You don't have to explain. I get it."

"No, I want to."

"Why?" I crossed my arms and studied his expression. Was this about trying to save face? Save our...relationship, whatever it meant to him? There was so little time and so much uncertainty.

He raked his hands through his hair. "Because...everything I want to say isn't....I really like you and I don't want to screw this up, but I feel like everything I do and say is wrong."

He sat up and leaned over, as if willing me to understand.

"I'll admit, I came for Holly, and my sister and I didn't want to get distracted. But you do weird things to my brain, Bethany. In a good way. Why I ever thought listening to Holly's lectures was more important than spending time with you, I'll never know."

He was about to kiss me. His lips were so close. Part of me wanted to push him away, but I also wanted to grab his shirt and pull him in. Decisions, decisions. He was going to break my heart. Smatter it in a way Todd was never capable of. How was this possible?

My hormones overtook my frazzled brain and I lunged for him, pressing my lips to his. I was a mushy, tingly mess, sighing as he pulled away briefly to stroke my hair and kiss my forehead. He grinned, before returning his lips to my mouth.

CHAPTER 17

Carter took me aside at the cocktail party, leaning over to whisper in my ear. "I'm voting for you tonight."

"You can't. You promised Holly."

"Before we came here, we talked about the possibility one of us would meet someone. We agreed all bets would be off if that happened."

"Then she knows?"

"Yes. She threw things. She screamed. She made sure cameras came over and caught her tantrum. America will not forget her. If she wants it, I'm sure she'll have a great acting career after this."

"But Carter, you have to know it's not all an act. She's in love with you. If she puts the moves on you here, on this show, and you reject her, she can claim she was only acting. Friendship still intact. It's brilliant, actually."

"No way."

"Yes way. Think about it."

Greg tinged his glass. As we walked over to the conference room, the butterflies in my stomach turned into bats. Carter was voting for me? If Holly didn't find a way to murder me before leaving tonight, this could change everything. All day long she'd monopolized Carter's time, as if she knew it was the last day she'd get with him. Dave kept me away, torturing me with lengthy interviews where I had to lie about almost everything. Except for exchanging a few longing glances, this was the first conversation we'd had since yesterday. And to be honest, that hadn't been much of a conversation once we started kissing.

As we reached the conference room, I immediately noticed the lack of furniture. Except for some mats arranged in a circle on the floor, everything was cleared out. Each mat had a name monogrammed on it. I glanced at Jada and she gave me the longest eye roll known to mankind.

I found the mat with my name scrolled on it and sat down. Tyson's mat was next to mine and he sat down and squeezed my hand.

"Is this some kind of yoga thing?" he asked. "Sounds hot."

Greg clapped his hands twice to grab our attention. "The theme for elimination night is Duck, Duck, Goose."

I dropped my head in my hand, but not before catching Jada giving Dave a hand gesture to let him know what she thought of this.

"On your turn, you will walk around, declaring each contestant a duck, until you reach your goose." He winked. "Usually, the goose does the chasing, but in our game, you will chase your goose around the circle and give them a kiss, signifying your choice."

There were several groans in response, and then, after a lecture about our bad attitudes, Greg gestured for Eddie to start. We sat through Eddie choosing Sylvie and then Sylvie picking him back. There was lots of giggling, fake running and syrupy kisses. Blech.

At least Jada put up a real effort to sprint around the circle before Marco caught her. Her competitive nature kicked in, even when it came to Duck, Duck, Goose.

Michelle and Patrick finally got to choose each other, having run out of other options.

My stomach was in knots when Carter stood up to take his turn, but he gave me an encouraging nod before starting around the circle, lightly touching each head. He paused when he reached Holly and she closed her eyes.

"Duck."

He continued around the circle until his fingers rested on my head.

"Goose."

I scrambled off the floor, my shoes sliding and I waved my arms to keep my balance before taking off in a run. I could hear Carter laughing behind me and he caught me easily, lifting me off my feet and up into his arms.

"Will you be my goose this week?" he asked, his eyes twinkling down at me.

I smiled and nodded, sure my whole face was red as he bent down and kissed me. It was a sweet, soft kiss that only lasted a moment, but he seemed to breathe me in before pulling back.

Of course, Greg asked Holly to go next. Dave needed the tension for the cameras. I just hated the tension it was creating for me.

Holly's eyes grew hard and determined as she got up and started making ducks. She slapped harder than everyone else, and gave my head a good whack as she went by. She reached Carter and slapped the side of his head. "Goose."

"Ow." Carter rubbed the spot and looked up at her. She waited with her arms crossed until he stood and slowly backed away. It was like watching an animal frozen in the cross-hairs of its prey, each waiting for the other to make the first move.

Finally, Carter feinted to the right and ran around her left. She spun and took off after him. He was going to make it to his mat, but she jumped onto his back and knocked him off balance, sliding them into Sylvie.

"Hey!" Sylvie pushed them off her and we scattered away from the mats while Holly flipped him over and pinned him to the floor. It's not like he couldn't have taken her in a wrestling match, but he was too much of a gentleman to handle a girl roughly, even if she deserved it. Dave was laughing his head off. So was Jada. Greg looked like he was about to cry. Train. Wreck. I shouldn't have let Carter vote for me.

Holly pushed Carter's shoulders into the floor and bent down for a kiss. Strangely, the scene reminded me of Sleeping Beauty, if the fairy tale had been a horror film. Carter lay uncomfortably still and Holly pressed her mouth to his, her hands moving to splay across his chest.

"Oh, help us now," Michelle murmured as the kiss seemed to go on and on. At first it was like watching her kiss a dead body, but then Carter sat up a little and wrapped his arm around Holly's back. My stomach dropped. They'd never kissed before, at least not like this. Maybe he felt something, because it looked like he was kissing her back. I didn't know what to do with my eyes, everywhere I looked brought pain, all the cameras recording, everyone's laughter, so I stared at a spot on the wall while Eddie and Marco wolf-whistled and hooted.

I so badly wanted to, but I couldn't run off. We weren't even done voting. All I could do was swallow, over and over again, holding back the urge to vomit, or cry, or both.

I snuck a glance and Holly finally came up for air, putting out a hand to help Carter to his feet. He looked sheepish. She looked smug, shooting me an evil smile. Even though she was going home, she'd made sure to cause as much trouble as possible before leaving. Man, I hated her so much.

It was Tyson's turn. Dang it. He was going to vote for me. I didn't want to run around again and have to kiss Tyson. I didn't think my legs would work and I still felt like I might be sick at any moment.

Tyson patted my back as he got up and started the other direction, meaning he'd reach me last. He was choosing me for sure. I tried to steel myself for this. *Happy. Feel happy. Don't look upset.*

"Goose!" Tyson grinned down at Holly. Her face scrunched up in both confusion and disgust. I thought she might refuse to get up, but she glared at him and launched herself off the floor, taking him by surprise.

Tyson laughed and ran after Holly, who looked both terrified and ticked off. She left the circle and zig-zagged out of his reach before he finally got his arms around her and pulled her into him. Their backs were to us, although a camera filmed them from the front. Holly grew still as Tyson whispered something in her ear, and then slowly she flipped around in his arms and gazed up into his face. She still looked mad, but I also saw nervousness and a little bit of anticipation. Really? My brain was going to explode.

Tyson bent down, kissing her soundly. She seemed to melt into him for a moment before stiffening and pulling away. "Enough already. I accept. I'm your goose. Whatever."

Tyson grinned. "Caught me a goose."

Holly flicked his ear and then stalked back to her spot on the floor. "You mean nothing to me," she called over her shoulder.

Tyson put his hand to his heart, as if she'd wounded him. "I'll grow on you baby. Just wait."

"Like a tumor," she said, rubbing his kiss off her lips.

"Bethany! You're up." I jumped at the sound of my name. I'd forgotten I still hadn't voted. People around me adjusted the mats and sat back down in our stupid circle while I tried to get my head to stop spinning. What was I supposed to do? Carter was safe. My vote didn't matter. Plus, the thought of kissing him now.... No. I couldn't even look at him.

Shakily, I got to my feet and went around touching heads. "You're not saying it, Bethany," Greg interrupted.

"Saying what? Oh." I started over and touched every head in the circle, saying 'duck' each time before realizing I was supposed to choose someone. So I went around again and stopped when I reached Tyson.

"Goose."

He'd tease me later for sounding so half-hearted, but right then I wasn't in the mood for jokes. Tyson jumped up and I jogged after him, waiting until he reached his seat again.

"Glad you're still with us," I said, reaching down and giving him a peck. He touched my cheek, worry in his eyes.

"Thanks, Bethany. I love you, doll."

I heard at least one gasp, but I knew what he meant. I didn't have to keep him. Because of Tyson, Holly was staying, and while I was mad about it, mostly I was heartsick, something Tyson had nothing to do with.

CHAPTER 18

Fueled by anger, hurt and frustration, I left the conference room in a fast walk. If I ran, someone would follow, wanting to know if I was okay, and I was totally not. So I power-walked instead, doubling back when I was way ahead of everyone and heading for the tool shed.

A flashlight would have come in handy, but even the thought of spiders didn't stop me from flinging the door open and inching my way over to the left side until I found the drivers and golf balls from my date with Carter. Working my way out of there with a heavy bucket of balls and a driver was trickier. I knocked over a lawn trimmer, cringing at the loud crash. After a minute of quiet, I closed everything up and took off with my loot.

The stairs up to the roof were behind the hot tub where Jada and Marco were sitting, having stripped down to swimwear in record time (I hoped they were in swimwear—It was dark and I didn't look too closely).

Betting on their indifference to my night activities, I climbed the stairs as quickly as possible and took in a deep breath at the top. The quiet, starry night was exactly what I needed. I walked to the edge of the roof and stared up, finding the few constellations I knew. Up here, it didn't hurt so much. There was life outside this dingy apartment complex and it would go on, regardless of Carter...no, I couldn't think about him yet...regardless of what scheme Dave cooked up next.

It had been the craziest elimination night by far, and nobody even went home. My boss would be happy. As bad as a love triangle would be, I was stuck in the middle of a love square. Nobody would care about Sylvie and Jada getting back together with their exes. Michelle and Patrick ignored each other on camera. No, all the attention, all the drama, surrounded me. Mom would be so pleased.

Picking up the driver and golf balls, I headed over to the little turf platform. I almost felt sorry for the little white ball as I lined it up and rolled the driver between my hands. It was about to take the brunt of my hostility.

Thwack. It sounded so satisfying. Five more balls arched out, whistling in the night air before landing in the desert.

"Can we try?"

I whirled around at the intrusion, my golf club raised in defense.

Jada laughed. "Whoa, girl. We'll leave if you still need your space. Looks like fun though."

Marco nodded, hands in his bathrobe pockets. "I love golf."

I lowered my weapon and held it out. "Who's next?"

"Ooh. Me!" Marco's hand shot up like an eager pupil and I climbed down to let him take his turn.

Jada tugged her towel tighter around her chest. "You sure can pick em, Bethany."

"What?"

She turned to look at me. "Men. Todd, clearly a bad apple. But let's not talk about him." She shuddered. "He's the crud you wipe off the bottom of your shoe."

If she didn't want to talk about Todd...

"So I get that a square like Carter is totally your style. But with Holly's claws in him...she's like the clingy mother-in-law he'll keep apologizing for and inviting over. If you want him, you'll have to make him get rid of her."

We heard noise on the stairs and turned to see Eddie and Sylvie coming up. Great. It was only a matter of time before the cameras followed.

"Bethany came up here to be alone. We already crashed her party. What do you guys want?"

Wow. Jada could get away with being rude to anyone.

Sylvie glared at her. "Eddie wants to hit balls off the roof. Don't you, babe."

Eddie looked like he wasn't so sure now. Gatekeeper Jada's

stance was pretty intimidating.

"Let him over, Jada." Marco called. "I wanna see if he can hit farther than me."

That left the three of us standing together awkwardly.

"Where's Bert and Ernie? Is the camera crew following you?" Jada asked.

Sylvie shook her head. "They were filming Michelle and Patrick confessing their love for each other on camera. Whatever. I needed air." She picked at her hair and sighed. "I need a trim. And a manipedi. I came on here because I wanted to be treated like a star, not like…the help."

Jada made a noise like a harrumph. She was likely thinking the same thing, but would never admit it.

"So is he, like, the real thing, or are you just passing the time?" Sylvie nudged her chin towards Marco.

Jada put her hands on her hips. "The real thing. What about you?"

Sylvie pursed her lips. "I'd rather not say."

Jada smirked.

My head hurt. I was about to bow out, when there was noise on the steps again. One set of feet. Our three heads turned to look.

The sight of Carter pushed my heartbeat into overdrive. Mutinous heart.

"Bethany, I've been looking for you."

I nodded and studied my ugly green flats with ribbon detail. I'm not sure who deserved death more, the person who designed them, or the person who put them in my closet.

"Bethany?"

"She's not happy with you right now." Jada took a step in front of me and I hated myself for letting her. This was supposed to be my fight.

"Duh," Sylvie added, giggling to herself.

Carter tried to step around Jada. "Please talk to me, Bethany. What's the matter?" He reached out for my hand, but I shook my head. The reason I'd gone to the roof was to get some time to think. I wasn't ready for this conversation. Unfortunately Jada lived for conversations like this.

"The matter is," Jada snapped, "you should have pushed that red-headed maniac off of you. What were you thinking? You can't have it both ways, Casanova."

Carter's shoulders slumped. "She was going to sucker fish my face until I responded, so yes, I kissed her back. To be honest, it felt weird. She's like a sister to me."

Sylvie sniffed. "Poor Holly. I would die if my ex talked about me like that."

"He's lying, obviously." Jada put a finger in Carter's chest. "Try again."

"It's true. Look, I don't have to explain this to you." Jada's jaw set and Carter took a deep breath. "Jada, you're being a loyal friend. I get that. I am respectfully asking you to let me talk to Bethany. Alone."

"And I'm asking you to explain yourself." She stepped into his personal space, backing him towards the edge of the roof. Carter glanced behind him and the panic in his face jolted my frozen brain into action. They didn't know about his fear of heights.

"Jada, don't!" I ran and threw my arm around him, trying to ignore how gloriously wonderful he smelled, how it immediately conjured up memories of kissing him. I grabbed his sweaty hand (poor guy) and dragged him downstairs. He'd come to my rescue after I fell off the treadmill. I was simply returning the favor.

Dave and company were making their way over to the stairs.

"We're going to go change into swimsuits," I lied, pointing at the hot tub.

They let us go and we ran upstairs and into my apartment. The déjà vu from a few days ago was on my mind as the door closed behind us. I didn't flip on the light. No use cluing Dave into our location.

"You, sit over there. I'm sitting way over here. Don't try anything funny. Just listen."

Carter put his hands up. "Whatever you ask." He sat down where I directed and shook his head. "I didn't know what to do with Jada. All these aggressive women, I'm not used to it. My mom is pretty much the calmest, sweetest woman on earth. And I can't imagine my sister jabbing some guy in the chest."

"Or pinning him to the floor?"

Carter sighed, not saying anything for a while. We were in precarious territory and we both knew it. "Holly's not usually like this."

"When you said she's like a sister, did you mean it felt like kissing a sister, or that you two are that close?"

"Both."

His answer was reassuring and aggravating at the same time. Jada made it sound so easy, just get him to ditch her. It was about as likely as getting rid of the clingy mother-in-law she mentioned. And in either case, I was pretty sure Ask Abby would say it was his job, not mine.

I fingered a loose string on the couch. "So here's where I'm at, Carter. I like you." How much, he didn't need to know. "But you don't believe me when I tell you the truth about Holly. That's a problem. What I saw tonight was Holly embarrassing herself. Making a total fool of herself. Laying it all on the line, for you. And you're the hero. You couldn't let her down, let her epically fail after pining for you for so long. So instead of embarrassing her, you embarrassed me. You guys have known each other a long time. I can't compete with that kind of friendship. And I don't think I want to."

"But you don't have to compete. Holly and I are not going to date, ever. Not in real life. And she's not secretly in love with me. She was laughing about it afterwards. Thought the whole thing was hilarious."

Carter stared down at his hands. "I'm really sorry. Obviously, it wasn't funny to you. When you kiss Tyson, sometimes I want to question you about it, but I trust you. I know he's important to you in some way. I'm hoping like a friend, like I am with Holly. All this stuff in front of the cameras is fake. But I want what we have to be real."

He leaned forward like he was tempted to break the space between us, but I shook my head, warning him not to. "Real? Fake? Who knows anymore? Please, if you care about me, don't vote for me again. Let me go home."

Carter's face fell and we sat in silence for a while, listening to each other's frustrated puffs of air from across the room. The words had slipped out, but I didn't want to take them back. The risk of letting him back in my heart was too great. And what about when we went home? No. It was time to protect my heart.

CHAPTER 19

Dave, Greg and crew woke us bright and early the next morning. Greg's sunshiny voice started my headache anew. "Dress and eat a quick breakfast. You have a big day today, ladies! Pack your bags with clothes and toiletries to last a week. Then meet downstairs in thirty minutes."

Michelle jumped up and frantically started dashing around grabbing things. "Can you believe this? We're actually going somewhere. We should pack swimsuits."

I was not so optimistic. As we dragged our bags downstairs, I noticed crew going in and out of the other apartments, moving things. We were the last to arrive downstairs and Dave tapped his foot impatiently as we filled out the semicircle of contestants.

An assistant led Michelle over to Patrick, and Greg motioned for me to move next to Carter and take his hand. I snuck a glance at him as his warm fingers clasped mine. He gave me a cautious smile. "I have a bad feeling about this."

"Well my bad feeling could take yours in a fight."

He laughed at me, rubbing his thumb over my twitchy fingers. To say I was nervous was a gross understatement. Perhaps Dave had cameras in my head, because I stayed awake worrying about how to get to the next elimination night with as little contact with Carter as possible. Holding hands the next morning was definitely not in my plans.

Dave cleared his throat. "Since no one was eliminated last night, I'm going to have to reach in my bag of tricks to keep things interesting. I'll let Greg explain."

Greg stepped forward and graced us with his benevolent smile before turning to the cameras. "True love must stand the fires of time and trial. The couples you see before you must face a difficult task together, to see if their love is true."

An assistant came up and handed Greg a pink bundle. A very life-like cry escaped the blankets and we all glanced at one another in alarm.

"Caring for a baby requires selfless love and devotion. Let's see if our remaining couples can work together to make it a joy rather than a burden."

Greg turned the baby toward the camera. "This is a baby simulator, created to mimic the needs of a newborn. It will cry for a bottle, to be burped, to be rocked, or to have its diaper changed before it will calm and return to its sleep setting. Each couple will be given a doll, and will have to care for it until the next elimination night, which won't be for another seven days. Ladies, your bags are packed because you are moving into an apartment with your partner this week. You must stay in the apartment the whole time and work together as a team. Are you ready to be mommies and daddies?"

No, this was not happening. Seven more days, sleep deprived, and confined in an apartment with Carter. He turned and looked at me. His gaze held apprehension, but also a tiny bit of glee. He couldn't hide it. Last night, he'd agreed to give me space, but he hadn't been happy about it. I'm sure the wheels were already turning on how he could wheedle his way back into my good favor.

And Michelle thought we'd be going somewhere. We were more tied to this place than ever before.

"In addition," Greg added, eyeing us carefully, "We have removed the TV's from your apartments and you are not allowed to read books. The pantries and fridges will be fully stocked so you can make all your meals together. This special time will give the two of you a chance to either fortify the relationship, or decide if it should end for good. At the next elimination night, think carefully before you vote."

Jada immediately shook her head and refused to take the doll an assistant tried to hand her. "Uh-uh. No way. You give that thing to me and I'll lock it in a drawer and go back to the pool."

Dave took the doll from the assistant and shoved it under his arm. It was a good thing he wasn't going to be one of the fake parents.

"Obviously some of you need a bit of incentive." He glared at Jada. "The maker of these dolls is offering a five-thousand dollar prize to the couple who returns theirs in working order with the least recorded crying. You are representing their business, so we expect you to take this seriously. If you stay in the apartment and see this through, you'll each get five-hundred dollars, even if you don't win. Anyone who brings back a broken doll will pay for it, and these things are not cheap. A representative is going to come in and explain how they work, so pay attention. Any other questions before I send for her?"

Holly raised the hand holding Tyson's, forcing his arm up with hers. "Why am I paired with Tyson? I didn't vote for him. I should be with Carter."

Greg nodded sympathetically. "We understand how you feel, Holly. But we decided to go by the men's vote to determine teams for this week."

"That's sexist."

Dave walked over and leaned in her face. "Sorry, sweetheart. Real life is sexist, therefore, so is this show. Tyson voted for you. Go ahead and scream at him, but you'll look ridiculous, since he's the only reason you're not back home already."

"Errrahhh!" Holly released Tyson's hand and stomped her feet, her fists clamped so tight I thought retractable claws might burst out of them.

"But…" Dave stroked his chin. "I could give you an incentive. One that's only for you."

Holly froze, her head tilted ever so slightly as we waited for Dave to continue.

"If you and Tyson win, you'll get the five-thousand to split, but I'll also give you immunity, meaning you're guaranteed to stay another week, and, since I'm such a nice guy, you can choose a person to send home after everyone else votes."

"I can send anyone home, girl or guy?" She cast a quick glance at me.

Dave nodded. "Anyone."

"What about me?" Tyson asked. "Do I get that?"

Dave winked at Holly. "Nope. Just her."

So unfair. No wonder all these reality shows always had a token drama queen. They got all the perks.

I raised my hand. "You're forcing us into a compromising living situation."

Dave rolled his eyes. "You'll have twin beds, and a demanding baby to take care of. Finding time for romance is up to you. But if it makes you feel better, we are installing cameras throughout the apartments so you'll always have a chaperone. Is that better?"

He knew it wasn't, the slime ball, but I didn't want to push the issue, making everyone assume I feared Carter might be less than a gentleman. But a whole week... Just the touch of his hand was sending tingly danger messages to my brain. Every time his arm brushed against mine I had to remind myself that more important things were happening than my overactive nerves.

My plans would have to be altered. Avoiding him until elimination night was now impossible. Convincing him not to vote for me was still a possibility. We might hate each other after a week stuck babysitting a doll. Carter's knuckles brushed across my leg. *Hate. Think about hate.*

Dave looked over at Jada. "And if you mess with the cameras you're ineligible for the five-thousand dollar prize so don't get any ideas."

Jada scoffed. "Whatever."

I noticed she'd taken the doll though, cradling the thing in her arms like it was made of gold. I could live without an extra twenty-five hundred dollars, but on the off-chance we won, Carter could use both of our winnings to help with his sister's medical bills. And it was still a lot of money, even if he wouldn't accept my half.

Dave motioned for an assistant to bring in the doll company representative and soon we were practicing changing diapers and properly supporting heads. The final nail in the coffin came with the tracking bracelets placed around our wrists, matching us to our doll. Now whenever it cried, the thing would be waiting for one of us to wave our magic bracelet in its face and tend to its every need.

Dave came over, smirking at our solemn faces. "Carter, hurry upstairs and pack your bags. Tyson and Holly will be using your apartment. We've set you and Bethany up in Anna and Gretchen's old apartment."

As soon as Carter left, Holly shoved her doll at Tyson, her translucent blue eyes locking on me. "Hold this, I need to go talk to Bethany."

What did she want? The representative was in the middle of explaining how the doll should be burped. Holly came up next to me, smiling a big fake smile until the representative finished talking.

"You are so gone after this week."

I shrugged. "Great. I'm ready to go. The only reason I'd even try to win would be to help Carter with his family's medical bills."

Holly huffed out an annoyed breath, lifting her bangs. "Five thousand is like a drop in that debt bucket. They should declare bankruptcy and be done with it already. Did you know he personally paid for his sister to have her eggs harvested before her chemo? She may never need them, and it's like a ten percent chance it would work anyway, but that wiped out his savings. He needs to start thinking about his own future."

"Shh." She didn't seem to care if the cameras heard, but I did.

"Yeah, yeah. Secrets." Holly gave me one last dismissive glance and headed up to her room with Tyson. He'd made his bed in crazy town and now he'd have to lie in it. He hadn't been his regular jokey self all morning.

***

I couldn't get Holly's taunting words out of my head. She probably hated the irony of Carter's character—a poor man made poorer because he couldn't stop giving to others. It only made me like him better. But that was bad. Even if we made it past all the reality TV nonsense, which was not happening, long distance relationships were hard. Traveling when you don't have any money, impossible.

Plus, Holly would be there, a short drive away, scheming, pretending to be his friend. Nope, this relationship, if you could even call it that, was doomed. I would be better to face the reality now.

Carter put his hand on my shoulder, our pink-clad doll tucked in the crook of his other arm as we stood in the doorway. "I know you're not happy about this. So let's be brutally honest with each other."

"You start."

"I'm a man. If I'm going to be locked in an apartment with you for a week, I'm going to need things to do. Otherwise, I'll start following you around like, 'hey baby' and you're going to make me sleep outside."

I turned to look at him and a snicker escaped. The pure honesty in his expression was too much. I covered my mouth, afraid I'd start laughing and never stop.

"What?"

I shook my head, forcing myself back to calm before I tried to speak. "That conniving, slimy..."

"You're not talking about me are you?"

"No. Dave. You hit the nail on the head. He wants us to either smolder with passion, or drive each other so nuts that we can't stand the sight of each other. And if we give him both, even better. I say we turn the tables on him."

"I'm liking this. How?"

"I don't know. But let's agree right now. No drama. We'll take care of the baby, be pleasant with each other and bore the cameras to death. We're good at that."

Carter chewed on his bottom lip. I'd noticed he did it whenever he was concentrating on something. "Agreed. But I don't want to be bored, either. Holly wheedled a deal out of Dave. I say we go through the apartment, systematically, and come up with a list of demands. Things we'll need to stay sane."

If lists made him feel better, I was game. We checked the pantry and fridge first and wrote down a few items we'd need for baking. Carter wanted Dr. Pepper. I decided to ask for better coffee.

They'd left us a stack of board games, but we decided to ask for Risk and Monopoly, two great time fillers.

The doll started howling and Carter ran over to pick it up. He fumbled with the fake bottle, trying to hold it in the right position, but the doll continued to cry. I sat down next to him on the couch and pulled out the color-coded diapers they gave us.

"Let me try." Carter handed me the doll and after exchanging diapers, the doll began to coo and then went silent.

"That was amazing." Carter grinned at me, sliding a strand of hair behind my ear and kissing my forehead.

Instinctively I scooted back from him, tucking my legs up and wrapping my arms around them. "Nope. You can't do that. No kissing."

Carter leaned back against the couch, his eyebrows coming together in a worried line. "It was a platonic gesture, Bethany. I'm sorry." He was looking at me as if I'd lost my mind, and maybe I had. Ten minutes into this, I'd already broken my own rule: no drama.

He stared down at the doll between us on the couch. The silence continued, getting more and more awkward.

"So let's talk about boundaries," he suggested.

I resisted smacking myself in the forehead and took his hand instead. "Let's not. Let's just win this thing, and I'll try not to bite your head off every time you talk to me."

Carter looked down at our hands. "I care about you, Bethany. So much it scares me. And I know you're scared, too—"

"How about that list?" I jumped up and ran over to the pad of paper we left on the counter. "I'm adding a jump rope. The staff apartments are on the bottom level. If we can't sleep, neither should they."

CHAPTER 20

Carter kept his distance after that. In fact, he apologized every time our hands brushed as we handed off the doll, or when we bumped into each other making lunch in the tiny kitchen. We barely spoke.

The crew interrupted us in the afternoon for interviews and Dave reluctantly took our list, glancing over it with an irritated, dismissive look on his face. "Chewing gum, yes. Noise-cancelling headphones? Not on your life." He folded up the paper and stuffed it in his pocket.

I thought about throwing myself on the floor and having a massive tantrum. Maybe then I'd get what I wanted. Unfortunately, personal dignity still ranked higher than snacks or headphones.

They let me out of the apartment for my interview with Greg. Two chairs sat in the hallway, a few feet from our door. Even so, fresh air and a break from the awkward tension with Carter made the intrusive, repetitive questions slightly less annoying.

"How do you feel about Carter?"

The same as yesterday. He's unbearably, deliciously attractive, kind, funny, and totally unattainable, at least in the long term. "He's fun to be around, Greg. We enjoy spending time together."

"Well, we've been watching the camera footage and it seems to me like you're mad at him. Or maybe he's mad at you? What's going on in there?"

It took all my concentration not to react to his question. How could they expect us to act natural if they were going to snoop on us and then quiz us on it? Greg's mouth curved up slightly. He knew he'd rattled my cage. *You…you smarmy donkey's bottom! You wish I'd fill you in.* "Throwing us together as roommates was unexpected. It will take some getting used to."

Greg raised an eyebrow. "Can you give us more?"

Oh yes, I'm dying to give you all the lurid details. Not that there are lurid details… Darn it, mind. Back on topic. "We're going to use this time to explore our relationship and see if we're compatible."

"What about Holly? She told us she'll use her vote, if she wins, to get rid of you."

Ugh. Yes, let's talk about Holly. She needs more attention. "I'd miss the show, of course."

"Of course." Greg patted my knee. He always acted like his role as host made him best buddies with everyone. "How are you feeling about Tyson, now that his attention has turned to someone else?"

I'd like to give him a good spanking, except he'd like that. I shrugged. "He has a thing for crazy redheads. To each their own."

"That's very fair of you."

"No use being jealous." *Dang it, why did I say that? They'd probably use that soundbite and pair it against every jealous thing I'd said or done on the show.*

I took my time after that, answering like a careful politician. My answers were boring and vague. It was my own way of sticking it to Dave and Greg. It made me feel better to think I did it on purpose. But the truth was, I didn't do well with interviews, I wasn't getting any better at it, and I'd have to go home and do more of these. Only on radio, they'd expect me to be funny. No careful editing or do-overs.

I went back inside the apartment and whipped up brownie batter and cookie dough, layering them in a muffin pan with an Oreo hiding in the middle.

Carter came in from his interview soon after, and the doll immediately started crying. I had messy hands, so I watched him try the bottle and then successfully burp the thing. Even in my bad mood, I couldn't help smiling. It wasn't every day you got to see a guy put a doll to his shoulder and pat it until it made a burping noise.

Carter walked over to peer in the batter bowls. "What are you making?"

"Slutty brownies. But don't get any ideas. They should be called post-interview brownies. I hate Greg."

"How can you hate Greg? He's like an adorable kitten."

"I hate cats."

Carter tried to hide his smile as he sidled up next to me. "Let me guess. You also hate puppies, nuns and Christmas."

He reached out to dip his finger in for a taste, but I slid the bowl behind me, daring him to try for it again. Wrong move. He stepped toward me and reached an arm around each side, pinning me to the counter, his face inches from mine. My heart hammered in my chest. He got his swipe of brownie batter and licked his finger, watching me with those serious, steel-blue eyes as if to ask, what are we going to do now?

The oven timer dinged and I let out a whoosh of air, pushing past him to pull the brownies out of the oven. I bustled around, doing everything except meeting his gaze.

This was why we couldn't afford to get comfortable with each other. Because when we did, we got too comfortable. One normal conversation where Carter tried to cheer me up and we're seconds away from making out.

And the cameras! I'd forgotten all about them. Everything I'd said about Greg, every tension-laced glance, all caught on film. I rubbed a hand across my forehead and took a bite of brownie, barely tasting it. The most heavenly treat on earth couldn't distract me from the volleying emotions throwing my thoughts into chaos.

Carter ate three brownies, commenting to me how good they were, but our conversation had turned wooden and we went back to avoiding each other.

***

"You can't sleep with me next to you, can you?"

I snorted. "Don't flatter yourself."

Five minutes later I was ready to admit defeat. That dang doll was going to cry any minute and we were both staring at the ceiling, pretending we were okay with the sleeping arrangement.

"Any ideas?" I asked.

"You could come over here to my bed and snuggle with me."

"Any other ideas?"

"It was worth a shot." Carter turned over and punched his pillow down. He lay still for a minute before flipping over once again, a frustrated sigh escaping.

"I've got to be the worst roommate ever," I admitted aloud.

"Well, you're definitely the best-looking roommate I've ever had. And you bake. So that's a plus."

"But we're like friends with benefits, only you're not getting any benefits, and I'm being a terrible friend."

Carter sat up on one elbow. "Please don't take this the wrong way. I have no idea what you want."

What did I want? "I want things to be how they were before."

"Before what?"

Ugh. This is so hard. "When we could talk to each other, like normal people, without expectations or…or this awkwardness between us. Kind of like how I am with Tyson."

"You want me to be like Tyson?"

"That's not what I said."

Silence. *Darn it. We're not going back to that.*

I threw off the sheet, got up and sat on the edge his bed, forcing him to look at me. "I'm sorry. For everything. Tomorrow I'm going to wake up and be cheery, even if I'm exhausted. And I won't freak out if you do or say something flirtatious. And I won't ignore you or stop talking to you if something's bothering me. We'll go back to brutal honesty, like you said."

"Brutal honesty," he repeated, reaching out to run his hand down my arm. The doll started crying, but I ignored it, peering into his face. In the dark it was hard to gauge his expression. "My honest opinion is that you should go take care of her. Because otherwise I'm going to try to keep you here. I really do like to cuddle."

I gave him a playful swat and went to get the doll. Carter was asleep when I finished feeding the thing. With a large yawn, I climbed into my bed and knew I'd be asleep within seconds.

The sound of wailing jerked me awake, and I stumbled into the front room, fumbling for the light. The microwave clock read 4:30. Carter had the crying doll on his chest. His head was lolled back against the couch, mouth open, lightly snoring. How many times had he taken care of that thing? We were supposed to take turns.

I went over and eased the doll out of his hand so I could try to give it a bottle. Little sucking noises indicated I'd guessed correctly. After feeding the thing for ten minutes, it cooed. I reached out and gently shook Carter.

"You're going to have a stiff neck. Come to bed."

Carter moaned and squeezed his eyes tighter, throwing an arm over his face. I got up to turn out the light.

"Carter, come to bed."

"You don't want me in your bed."

"Funny. Not my bed. Go to yours, hot stuff."

He mumbled something incoherent and slid sideways down the couch. Giving up, I went to get him a pillow and tucked it under his head before taking the doll back with me. I awoke a few hours later with my arm wrapped around it like a stuffed animal.

A whistling sound led me to the kitchen and I found Carter standing at the kitchen counter whisking eggs. He winked at me as I self-consciously felt the back of my hair, which was lumpy and probably looked terrible. The doll began to cry. I took it over to the couch to go through the routine of trying the bottle, trying to burp it, changing its diaper, and then rocking back and forth. After five minutes, it finally stopped crying and went back to sleep mode.

"Do you mind if I go shower before breakfast?" I asked.

"I won't put the eggs in the pan till I hear you get out."

His eyes continued to follow me as I walked over to get the orange juice out of the fridge, like he was keeping tabs on my mood, in case it might change any minute. Great. I'd become unpredictable, and not in a good way.

I poured myself a small glass and snuck a glance at him. Still watching me. I had an insane urge to kiss him good morning. My bed hair was embarrassing, but his was adorable. Instead, I took a few small sips and ran to take my shower.

***

Carter studied the Risk board while balancing a bottle against the doll's mouth. "Our doll needs a name. I've heard you call her 'that thing' two times today."

I shrugged. "She's gone all week without a name. And what's wrong with calling her Thing? It worked for *The Addams Family*."

Carter raised an eyebrow. "That was for a creepy hand in a box. I'm naming her Bernice."

"That's worse than Thing."

Carter opened his mouth, pretending to be offended. "I named my first car Bernice. She's buried in a scrapyard somewhere. Her transmission blew up right before high school graduation."

I took a last delicious bite of my brownie. We'd given away most of our baked goods to the show staff, but there were still too many sitting on a plate on the counter. It seemed unlikely I'd be getting back in a bikini anytime soon.

"Fine. Call her Bernice then. And take your turn. My soldiers are going to die of old age before you can kill them off."

We were well into our third game. Risk was the best perk we'd gotten from Dave. There was little else in the box he brought to get excited about. I got my coffee. Carter got his Dr. Pepper and a couple decks of playing cards. They were on the end table, now in use as the biggest house of cards known to mankind. Carter and I were waiting to see how long we could go without knocking it down.

It had taken a few days to get into a rhythm, but spending all my time with Carter now felt normal and fun. More than fun. That word didn't encompass the contentment in me. I was glad I got to wake up and spend all my time with him. This realization scared me. A lot. The best way to handle it, I found, was to pretend I still didn't care what happened after this. Because if I didn't silence it, the time clock in my head would start ticking, reminding me this was all going to end soon.

"Earth to Bethany. I'm about to take over Africa. This better be an amazing dice roll for you."

I yawned and took my turn. Yep, I'd lost another continent.

"Let's call it a night." Carter slid the game board out of the way so we wouldn't trip on it in the dark and helped me up off the floor. "I'll take care of Bernice tonight. You're exhausted."

He kept my hand in his and laughed when I tried to conceal another yawn. As tired as I was, his touch still worked its magic on me, and I had to look away from him. It wasn't getting any easier, but I'd learned to bury those reactions, hide them away so I didn't encourage him. He didn't try to kiss me and I pretended I didn't notice how often he went out of his way to touch me, whether it was helping me up, or sitting close on the couch.

I looked at the pair of us in the bathroom mirror while we were brushing our teeth. Carter had circles under his eyes as big as mine. Thing was a demanding baby (Carter could call her whatever he wanted, to me she was Thing), but we were overtired from staying up talking. Because of the cameras, we avoided certain subjects, which was a shame. I had a mental list of things I wanted to know about Carter. And it grew every day.

CHAPTER 21

"Knock, knock, you two!"

Greg and a cameraman came in while we were making lunch.

"You might want to hold off on those sandwiches, because you're invited to a pool party playdate downstairs." Greg grinned at us like this was the best news ever, and technically it should have been. We hadn't been more than a few feet outside of the apartment in five days. But instead of elated, I felt annoyed. I liked sitting at the stools every day, eating lunch with Carter.

"You want us down there right now?" Carter looked at the massive pile of chips on his plate and frowned.

"Yes, now. I just left Sylvie and Eddie's apartment and they practically barreled me over to get outside. You two act like you don't want to leave." Greg wiggled his eyebrows and laughed. "Take your time, love birds, but all the catered Mexican food might be gone if you wait."

Carter glanced at me and shrugged. I pulled a box of plastic baggies out of a drawer and started putting food away.

"Oh, there are a few rules you must follow if you'd like to participate." Greg pulled out his list and read it off. "No touching any other couple's doll, no alcohol, no dolls in the pool, no leaving the pool area without permission, and most importantly, one of you must keep the doll with you at all times. You can switch off, of course, but no setting it down anywhere."

We nodded our agreement and Greg left to carry the good news to the other apartments.

A glance down at my current outfit told me I'd need a wardrobe change. My fuzzy pants and plaid button-down had been a choice born of comfort.

"I'm curious to see how everyone else is holding up." I closed the fridge and turned around to see Carter staring at me, worry etched across his face.

"Can we talk about going downstairs? I'm worried about you and Holly. She makes you crazy, makes you want to push me away. And I don't want that. I'll stay with you the whole time and not talk to her if it helps. Or if you're tired of me I'll leave you alone and keep her away from you. Whatever you want me to do."

In a perfect world, Holly wouldn't exist. But that wasn't fair. I'd promised him no drama. So even though the mention of her name made my lip curl, I would tame the jealous monster inside and not let her get to me.

"Carter, I want you to do whatever you think is best."

He looked at me like that was the worst answer in the world.

I took a step closer and stole a chip out of his hand. "I'm not tired of you."

***

All the other girls were in their standard bikinis, but it didn't make me regret my orange zebra-striped sleeveless blouse and matching orange zipper pants. I ran the outfit by Carter before we left and he laughed and told me it was eye-catching.

Dave did not look amused. He sent Greg over to tell me he'd failed to mention the dress code.

Feeling irritated, I handed Bernice over to Carter and ran upstairs. I figured Holly would pounce while I changed into a swimsuit, but when I came down again she was sitting in the same deck chair, staring at the doll on her lap.

Sylvie, however, had moved in next to Carter and was laughing at something he said like it was the funniest thing in the world. She put her hand on his arm and didn't move it away. In fact, she started rubbing.

Tyson came to stand next to me and crossed his arms, eyeing the situation. "I wouldn't worry. Carter's been checking the stairs every ten seconds to see when you'd come down. Eddie must have lost interest. Sylvie's back to her old tactics."

Part of me wanted to go rip Sylvie's arm off of him, but I talked my jealousy down and waited, watching. Carter nodded at something she said and then looked down at his arm like she might be infecting him with cooties. She giggled and withdrew her arm, but then slapped him in the chest and kept her hand there. Unbelievable. It was better not to watch. Besides, Carter wasn't mine. I had to keep telling myself that.

For the first time, I took in Tyson's appearance. He looked tired, but more than that, defeated. "How are you?"

Tyson stared at the ground, rubbing his toe against the pool deck. "Holly's insane. Like, certifiably. The only time she lets me take care of the doll is when she uses the bathroom or showers. And even then, only after she's fed and burped it so the chances of it crying are low. And the one time it did cry when I had it, she freaked out and burst out of the bathroom to take over."

"I'm so sorry."

"It's my fault. I thought it might be fun to put the moves on her, maybe lighten her up a bit. But she's got a laser focus on winning this competition and ousting you. If I were Carter I'd be afraid, very afraid. He should thank his lucky stars he's not rooming with her. I'd be terrified to fall asleep." He shivered. "She's scary."

"Well maybe you can talk to him about it. He still thinks she wants to be an actress."

Tyson threw back his head and laughed. "She could be. She could be anything she wanted to be. It just so happens, her one true desire is to be Carter's girlfriend."

Carter finally disentangled himself from Sylvie and walked over. "Hey Tyson, how's it going?"

They shook hands and I was about to give them a minute, maybe go chat with Jada and Marco, when Tyson touched my shoulder. "Hold on. You two should know, barring some terrible accident, and I'd be lying if said I hadn't considered creating one, Holly and I are going to win this. Yeah, me. Money. But that means Bethany's going home in two days and you're not." He looked at Carter and some kind of understanding passed between them.

Carter's hand reached out and found mine. "Thanks, Tyson."

"Tyson! Where is the diaper with the green tag? You have to go get it right now." Holly stomped over to us and pointed up the stairs. "I have to keep the doll down here. Dave said. Hurry, before

I need that diaper."

Tyson jogged up the stairs, shaking his head.

Carter stared at Holly, a disapproving look on his face. "You shouldn't talk to him like that."

She turned to smile at him and visibly relaxed. Within two seconds, the screaming shrew disappeared and sweet, friendly Holly replaced her. "Oh Carter, he knows it's for the cameras. You should see him boss me around sometimes. Living with him has been...interesting. I think I've finally got him cured of walking around in his underwear."

Her eyes flitted to our clasped hands. "You two figured out the long distance thing yet? That will all be on you, Bethany, since Carter hates flying. He only made it here by downing a few drinks before takeoff. I told the flight attendants he was sick and had them prepare a wheelchair for him when we landed. He was asleep on my lap."

Carter stared at the ground, shuffling his feet. "Thanks for sharing, Holly."

Holly blinked at him and crossed her arms. "Well, she should know these things."

"Thank you, but I already know about his fear of heights. Carter, is this a regular thing for you to get drunk and pass out on planes?"

"It was my first flight," he mumbled.

Tyson darted back down the stairs, pulling Holly's focus away from us. She grabbed the diaper from him right as their baby doll began to fuss. We watched her whip out a bottle from her pocket and stop the crying within seconds.

"Is it crazy that I want to go back upstairs already?" I asked.

Carter grinned at me. "Let's ask Dave how long we have to stay here."

***

Tyson and Holly had given us a lot to think about, but my plan to ignore the future had worked great so far and I wasn't about to abandon it. We needed stuff to do. Carter looked far too pensive. I suggested tackling the bathroom when we got back to the apartment and he agreed.

After changing out of our swimsuits, we grabbed the cleaning supplies and got to work. I swept and mopped the floor while Carter spritzed the shower and wiped it down. Carter wouldn't let me clean the toilet, so I worked on the counter and mirror while he did that.

"Do you think—?"

"What should we have for dinner?"

"I don't know." Carter looked at me funny. "We should exchange phone numbers."

"Spaghetti sounds good."

Carter frowned at me. "Bethany. I know what you're doing."

"And I know what you're doing. Stop letting Holly's meddling get to you. I don't want to talk about the F word."

"What? Future?"

I covered my ears like it was actually a bad word. To me it was. "Yes. And I'm not having this conversation while you scrub a toilet."

"Technically I'm done scrubbing. I'm wiping down the seat and lid." He turned to look at me. "And I think this is the perfect time. We can talk in here. It's the one place Dave can't stick a camera." He pushed the door closed and came over to the sink to wash his hands. I threw my cleaning wipe out, soaped up my hands and put them in the water with his.

Our eyes met in the mirror and his gaze told me all the things I wasn't letting him say. The towels were behind me and he reached around me to dry his hands. His head dipped down to meet my lips and I didn't stop him, in fact, my wet hands instinctively went up around his neck. I tried to murmur sorry, but his lips wouldn't let me.

His kiss was so fierce and sweet, all the buried emotions from the week bubbled up and overwhelmed me. I told myself I'd pull away at any moment, but it couldn't be this moment. Or this one. Or the next one. But it was Carter who pulled away and left the bathroom, giving me a mysterious smile. He came back in with a pad of paper and a pen.

"I wrote down my phone number. I want yours."

I took the notepad and pen from him while my mind whirled. How could I think clearly when my body was still buzzing head to toe from his embrace? "We're not supposed to contact each other until after the show airs."

"We're not supposed to be seen in public together. That's

different."

The thought of waiting for him to call or wondering if one day he'd just stop calling seemed worse than leaving with a clean break. Even though there was no such thing as a clean break. My heart was going to bleed all over the place either way. Better to stanch the bleeding early.

"So we call each other and then what? Holly is right. We have a long distance problem that's not going to go away." *She's not going away either.*

"You won't give me your number?" Carter wouldn't let me look away. He touched my cheek and stared into my eyes. "I have all these things I want to say to you and they whirl around my head at night. I go through all the possible consequences if I say them out loud and all the consequences if I don't say them. And then I think, I'll tell you tomorrow."

I didn't mean to shake my head. It happened without my permission. But Carter kept asking me to take my feelings down from the shelf I'd placed them on and look at them. They were in neat stacks, out of sight. I didn't want to pull them down and make a mess. Not until I was safely home, away from the cameras, away from Carter's hope-filled eyes.

"Don't say them. Not yet." I dropped my head into his chest and took my time breathing. It didn't feel automatic at the moment. I felt like if I didn't concentrate on taking air into my lungs, I'd forget and pass out.

Carter stroked my hair and sighed. "Why not?"

Because we're hopeless. Because if he said them here, they'd belong to the show, even if they weren't recorded. Bernice started crying and I moved to pull away.

"I'll get her," he said, giving me a mournful look.

CHAPTER 22

Agitated voices woke me. It was dark and I didn't even remember falling asleep. Had I slept for minutes, hours? What time was it?

"What do you mean, now?"

That was definitely Carter's voice. Who was he yelling at? My feet found the carpet and I stumbled over to the door and opened it. The light was on in the kitchen.

Dave and Greg stood there with a cameraman, fully dressed and awake. Dave had Bernice under his arm. I leaned against Carter and looked to him for an explanation.

"They decided to surprise us and do the vote now."

Dave nodded. "We've already looked at the data from the dolls. It's not even close. The winning couple has almost a half hour less of crying. We also have enough footage of everyone for this episode. More than enough. Let's move on, people." He gestured for us to walk in front of him.

"I have to pee," I admitted.

Dave sighed and held up his pointer finger. "One minute."

It was over. I might never see Carter again and his last view of me would be this...my weary reflection blinked back at me as I washed my hands. Dave banged on the door, yelling for me to hurry up. And then Carter yelled at him. So I dried my hands quickly and came out.

I was too tired to be embarrassed or even angry that Dave thought he could treat me like a prison inmate. Carter took my hand and we walked out of the apartment together. He leaned over to whisper something.

"No talking until after the votes," Dave barked.

Carter pulled a slip of paper out of his pocket and handed it to me. How did he manage to write me a message? But then I realized it was the phone number he'd written down for me. I'd left it on the pad, but he took it with us, knowing I might be leaving tonight.

I thought I'd wanted to go home, but that was when I had two more days here. There were so many things left unsaid. Although, maybe that was a good thing. We reached the conference room and Greg pulled me over to the chairs on one side of the room, while Carter followed Dave over to the men's side.

Michelle looked at me. "I think this is my fault. Patrick and I don't care about the money or staying here, so we're not voting for each other. We didn't even try to hide it from the cameras. Dave probably doesn't want anyone else planning their escape before elimination night." She glanced over at Sylvie, who sat picking at her nails, indifferent to the whole thing.

"You and Patrick are breaking up?" I'd hoped they'd work things out.

Michelle laughed. "Of course not. But now we have a plan. My sister and brother-in-law are renovating a triplex in Chicago and need help with the mortgage in a bad way. They have plenty of room for us. I have to put my condo up for sale and start job hunting."

She drummed her fingers on the edge of the chair, full of energy, even though we'd all been pulled out of bed.

"Patrick's accounting company opened up a firm in Chicago last year. They asked him if he wanted to transfer and he told them no. He's never had a reason to leave New Jersey before. But he's going home to tell them yes. It may take a few months, but we'll go ring shopping as soon as we both make it to Chicago and I'm...I'm so happy!"

She seemed to realize just then, that I might be going home too, but not with the glow and purpose driving her. "Oh, Bethany. Are you going to be okay? What are you and Carter going to do?"

"I don't know." I glanced across the room at Carter. He met my eyes, looking worried, but hopeful.

"Hey!" Dave was walking back in with Tyson and Holly, the last couple. "No talking." He glared at Michelle.

"See, I told you it's my fault," she whispered.

They did a hair and makeup check while pinning microphones to us. Since they wanted us to look disheveled and worried, that mainly consisted of ruffling hair and accentuating the circles under our eyes.

Greg stepped into the middle of the room to begin his customary speech. "This has been a trying week, testing your patience with the dolls, but also with each other. Some of you have drawn closer, worked together, and found joy in the experience. Others have not."

He paused and glanced from one side of the room to the other, studying our faces. "I will not reveal the winning couple until after the voting so as not to influence your decision. We are handing out paper and pens. Please quickly write down the name of the person you are voting for on a slip of paper, fold it, and hand it in."

Michelle shifted uncomfortably in the seat next to me. She probably thought the secret ballot was her fault, too. Perhaps Dave would edit the footage to make it look like they'd broken up. Or maybe he'd add their names in and make them stay. Unethical, but I wouldn't put it past him.

I glanced at Tyson and he gave a small shake of his head. He was ready to go. So I wrote down Carter's name, knowing it didn't matter with Holly voting for him, too.

Dave and a few assistants came over to look over the votes and plan the order Greg would announce them, while we sat and waited. Dave raked his fingers through his hair, occasionally turning to glare at us. There must be a lot of us leaving. We were supposed to be here for eight episodes and this was the end of episode four.

"Who'd you put?" I whispered to Michelle out of the corner of my mouth. I didn't want to catch Dave's attention and get yelled at.

"Carter. Oh, and Patrick's voting for you."

Dave turned to glare at us and I sank lower in my chair like a kid in detention.

Greg clapped to get our attention. "Okay, let's begin." His gaze swept over us as he held up the slips of paper. "When I call your name, please stand. Carter, four votes for you to stay. Marco, one vote. Bethany, three votes, Jada, two votes." He tisked and glanced at those still sitting. "The rest of you did not receive any votes."

An assistant brought Greg an official looking envelope and he held it up. "I will now reveal the couple with the least recorded crying and the winner of a fabulous five-thousand dollar prize."

Not Holly. Not Holly.

"Holly and Tyson, congratulations! Holly, please stand up with those staying and tell us who you choose to send home."

Jada whispered "unfair," and Holly turned to glare at her. But she wouldn't send Jada home. She looked back at me and smirked. "Bethany's leaving."

Greg nodded, and then continued. "Well then. Holly and Carter, Jada and Marco, we're so glad you're staying because we have an extraordinary adventure for you."

He shook his head at the rest of us, like a disappointed parent.

"Holly and Carter, Jada and Marco, your love once fizzled out, but over the next two weeks you'll have a second chance at love and fortune. You'll get to compete for a fabulous prize: a modeling contract with Patrician Diamonds. The winning couple will star in all their ads for the next year, showing off an amazing $50,000 engagement ring and other jewelry. The two of you will get paid $10,000 each up front, and a set amount for every commercial and print ad, depending on the success of the campaign. They will also let the lucky bride drip in diamonds on her wedding day, and turn that into a photo spread sold to several major magazines."

"I've never heard of Patrician Diamonds," Jada said.

"Exactly." Greg grinned. "After this, everybody will."

Carter's eyes met mine and he shook his head. "I won't do it," he mouthed.

Sylvie jumped out of her chair. "I've changed my mind. Eddie and I want to stay and work on our relationship."

Dave's eyes narrowed. "Too late. Holly, Carter, Jada and Marco, stay here with me. The rest of you follow Greg out for parting interviews."

"What about goodbyes?" Carter made a move to walk towards me, but Dave stepped in front of him. "We're skipping them."

***

My parting interview was a disaster. I couldn't focus on the questions, and at one point, started crying and couldn't stop. The knowledge that my breakdown was being recorded only made me cry harder.

They gave me fifteen minutes to change into my own clothes

and pack up my things from both apartments. Then they sent me down to one of the two sedans taking us to the airport. I got in the sedan with Tyson, Michelle and Patrick. We could hear Sylvie and Eddie screaming at each other as we pulled away from the curb.

I stared at my plane ticket in one hand, and my phone in the other. It felt strange to have it back.

Tyson was sitting in the front, next to the driver and he leaned back and took the phone out of my hand. "I'm going to put my number in here. My phone's dead, so write yours down for me." He handed me a pen and his plane ticket.

The irony stabbed me in the gut as I wrote my number down and handed Tyson his ticket back.

"What are you going to do when you get home?" I asked.

Tyson shrugged. "Deposit my check for twenty-five hundred dollars. Look for a new job. I was a telemarketer before this. I'm great at it, but it's the worst job ever, as bad as everyone says it is. I'm kinda hoping I can use my five seconds of fame, you know, once the show airs, to become a paid public speaker. I can warn everyone about the perils of dating or something."

"That sounds awesome. I'd come to listen." I smiled at him, but he looked down at my wringing hands.

"You have to have some faith in Carter. He's not going to marry Holly for money. He wouldn't do that."

"That's not what I'm worried about," I lied. I'd met Carter two weeks ago. Holly had been friends with him since kindergarten. I wasn't about to underestimate her. She'd managed to keep his friendship this long, she must have more tricks up her sleeve. "I'm worried about my job. My boss wants me on our radio station, spilling all the inside details about the show. I'm usually the one making commercials. I don't want to be one. You've seen me do interviews. I'm terrible."

It felt good to put my mind into something else. If I started thinking about Carter and Holly I'd drive myself batty.

"Bethany, your interviews are bad because you're too busy editing yourself. Take the filter off and be you. Don't apologize or sidestep anything that happened here. You're going to act like this was the best time of your life and you can't wait to talk about it. And do that interview after interview until you believe it. And then you can get back to your desk and do your thing."

"You really should be a motivational speaker, Tyson."

He took a little bow and then yawned. "If you don't mind, I think I'll take a nap."

I glanced at my phone. 5:45 a.m. Sleep would be an escape, but my mind was too wired to go there. The 2,600 unread emails, thirty-eight unread text messages, and seventeen missed calls didn't even tempt me to reengage with my life. This was what I wanted. I'd left the show, left Carter behind. But I'd left my heart with him. That wasn't part of the plan. Next to me, Michelle and Patrick cuddled and whispered together. I shivered, even though I wasn't cold, and stared out the window at nothing.

CHAPTER 23

If Mom asked, I planned to tell her she was my first call. But I called Katelyn first. I had to talk to her.

"Bethany? You got your phone back! Are you home yet?"

"No, I'm at LAX waiting for my flight. You sound out of breath. Are you okay?"

Katelyn's laugh turned into a grunt of pain. "Well, my water broke and Doug and I are on our way to the hospital. I only answered because it was you."

"Oh my. I'll let you go."

"No, you have to tell me everything. Oh, ow. It will help take my mind off the pain. How was it?"

I could not stress her out while she was going into labor. But Carter's face flooded my mind and tears pricked my eyes. "I met someone, but it's complicated."

"Isn't it always? Complicated how?"

"He's still there, with another girl. She got rid of me. I'll explain the voting stuff later."

Katelyn was repeating everything I said to Doug. "Doug says guys only go on shows like that for one thing."

"Well tell him we didn't do anything."

"Should I put you on speaker?"

"No."

I could hear Doug laughing. This was a bad idea. They didn't understand the situation at all. "Plus, there's the long distance problem. He's afraid of flying."

"Oh, no. Like he told you he's afraid of flying? Don't go see him. This might be Todd all over again."

"He's nothing like Todd. And he's really afraid of flying. It's not an excuse. There's a back story to that, but..."

"Bethany, we're pulling up to the hospital. I can't wait to hear the rest of it. Ow, I want drugs now."

"We'll talk about it later. Get your little guy out safely. Love you."

"Love you, too."

I ended the call and stared at my phone, wondering why I was defending a relationship I'd chosen to give up on. But how could I be hopeful about a reality TV romance when everyone else assumed it was nothing special? I pictured Carter's serious face when he handed me his phone number. It hadn't felt like nothing.

I reached into my pocket, but it was empty. Then the realization hit me. I'd left the slip of paper with Carter's number in the hideous orange zipper pants I'd left behind.

***

There were many sympathetic looks thrown my way, but none of my seatmates on the plane bothered me as I cried and twisted my wet tissues in my lap. I don't know why it mattered so much that I'd lost the piece of paper. I hadn't planned on calling him. But he'd pinned all his hopes on it.

After landing in Phoenix, I hailed a cab, looking forward to dropping in my own bed in my little rented house. There were so many things I'd taken for granted: cute clothes, privacy, no one to share a bathroom with…Even though sharing a bathroom with Carter hadn't been bad. Darn it. Not again. I wiped my nose and hugged myself, forcing the tears back.

As the cab pulled up to my house, I noticed a light on I could have sworn I'd left off. But then, I'd asked Katelyn to check on the house, so maybe she'd turned it on.

The cabdriver lugged my bags up to the front step and then drove off. I fumbled around in my purse for my keys, just as the door started opening from the inside. Who was in my house? It couldn't be Katelyn and Doug.

I took a step back and grabbed the pepper spray I kept in the bottom of my purse as the door opened.

"Put the mace away, Bethany. Don't you check your text messages?"

A whoosh of air emptied from my lungs as I took in Ryan's amused face. He shouldn't be laughing at me when he'd been two seconds away from blinding pain.

"What's the difference between a well-groomed monkey and a guy on reality TV? Yeah, I read that message. Hair gel. Very funny." I'd been in no mood to read more teasing messages from my brother.

Ryan grabbed my suitcase off the porch and brought it inside. "The message before that. I told you I was crashing at your place for a little while."

His face had turned much more serious, and for good reason. He had a wife. There was no reason for him to be staying with me when he had his own place a few minutes away.

"What's going on?" I asked as I checked the ramen noodles cooking on the stove. I hadn't left much food in the house, but clearly Ryan had been making do.

"Jasmine asked me to leave."

The hurt in his voice said more than his words. "When?"

"A week ago. She won't take my calls and I'm reaching a point where I don't want to keep trying. Especially after what she's done."

I poured the soup into a bowl and placed it in front of him at the table before turning to make another package for me. He shook his head and tried to offer me the soup, but I insisted and he relented.

"What did she do, Ryan?"

He sighed and stared at his bowl. "You remember at the wedding, one of her bridesmaids was a bridesman?"

I nodded. "Yeah. I assumed he was gay."

Ryan shook his head. "I wish. They've been friends since college. She said they were just friends. He had a girlfriend so I didn't worry too much about it. But he broke up with her about a month ago and Jasmine's been spending a lot of time 'consoling' him."

"Oh no."

"She swears nothing is going on, but that doesn't make it okay for me. She meets him for lunch at a café across from his work every day and they text constantly. Last Friday, that's when we had our big blowup. She came home at 1:30 in the morning, after going to dinner with him. I told her she had to drop him. She said she hadn't done anything wrong and told me to get out. So I left."

I added the seasoning packet to my soup, taking my time before responding. It was such a precarious situation. I didn't want to say anything I'd regret if they got back together. As much as I disliked Jasmine at the moment, I hoped they could work it out.

"You're not wrong. You should be the most important person in her life. Are you putting her first? Do you still play video games all day Saturday?"

He glared at me. "I did that in high school after I got cut from the track team for my grades. I've grown up since then."

It was hard to see Ryan as grown up. He'd always be my annoying little brother. "It's only been a week. I don't think it's time to give up. Stay as long as you want." *I have plenty of room and who else needs me? Right now, nobody.*

Ryan dipped his head down, twirling his soup spoon. "Thanks Bethany. I won't stay forever, I promise. I just can't rent an apartment. That would be like admitting it's over."

He put his bowl in the sink and rinsed it out as I sat down with my soup.

"Shouldn't you be at work right now?" I asked.

"I need a root canal. My appointment's in about forty-five minutes. My boss said to take a sick day."

"Quite the week you're having."

He looked at me as if suddenly realizing something. "You're back from your reality show. I've been blathering on about me and haven't even asked you about it."

My phone vibrated and a picture of a scrawny newborn popped up. The perfect distraction. After Katelyn and Doug's reaction, I was hesitant to explain anything about the show to Ryan.

"Oh! Look at this. It's Katelyn's baby."

Ryan smiled at the pictures and then went into the guest bedroom to get ready for his appointment.

"Don't you need someone to pick you up?" I asked. "I don't know if you should be driving after a root canal."

Ryan shook his head. "My friend Nathan said he would. He lives right by the dentist's office."

"Well, have fun."

Ryan grimaced. "Looking forward to it."

After he left, I showered and climbed into bed with a package of cookies, my thoughts in overdrive. It would be bad to sleep now, in the middle of the day. But I wasn't sleeping, I was hiding.

At what point does friendship cross a line? Before meeting Carter, maybe I would have sympathized with Jasmine a little. It shouldn't matter if a close friend was a guy or girl. But that only worked in theory, not in real life. Friendships were important. But more important than the person you love? Was it wrong to want Carter all to myself or not at all?

I knew I'd be thinking about him for a long time. Years from now, something would remind me of him and he'd pop into my mind, giving my heart a twinge. I should have never gone on that stupid show.

***

After Ryan got back, I forced myself out of bed and got dressed. He wasn't so drugged up that he wouldn't notice my catatonic state after a while.

I decided to make a list of things to do so I wouldn't go insane. It would be nothing like the list Carter and I made together. For one, I was back in the real world, with a job and bills and a life. Secondly, there was no boss I had to beg things from. I was the boss now, and it was time to put on my big girl panties and stop moping.

1. Call work and let them know I'll be in on Monday
2. Visit Katelyn. Explain Carter Try not to talk about Carter
3. Pick up mail
4. Buy groceries – get popsicles for Ryan
5. Purge house of cookies and chocolate, except for my emergency stash
6. Call Mom

I got everything done on my list in the exact order I wrote it. There was a reason I put 'Call Mom' last. Unlike Ryan, she couldn't take a gentle hint and turn the topic of conversation to other things. Mom would pry until she figured out what was bothering me. Oh, how I didn't want to talk about Carter with her. But I didn't have to. She hadn't seen the show yet. With that reassuring thought, I dialed her number.

"Hi Mom."

"You're back! I'm afraid to ask. How did it go? You didn't lose your heart to some hunk did you?"

"No, of course not." *Kill me now.* I hadn't planned on raiding my emergency chocolate stash, but I walked into the kitchen and climbed up on the counter to reach the glass jar I kept on the top shelf. Ryan watched me with amusement from his sickbed on the couch.

"So tell me about the other girls there. Did you make any friends? Or were they mean to you? I've been watching The Reality Network while you've been gone so I know all about the mean girls on shows like this."

"Some were mean and some were nice."

"Well yes, but which ones? What were their names?"

I soldiered on and told Mom how everyone suspected everyone else was acting, and how Jada told us her man was off limits. She ate up everything I said, and after a few minutes I relaxed, realizing this was great practice for going on the radio. No DJ could be more thorough than Mom.

"I'm worried about Ryan," she said after a while.

"You're worried about Ryan?" I repeated, glancing over at him.

He shook his head and made waving motions, mouthing "I'm not here!"

"I'm sure Ryan's fine."

"He's not answering my calls, so I called Jasmine and she very brusquely told me he probably didn't want to talk to me right now and hung up."

Ryan was looking at me expectantly, but I couldn't concentrate on filling him in and lying to Mom at the same time. I turned away from him and pried the lid off the candy jar.

"How could he marry someone so selfish? She's always in a bad mood and I don't think she treats him right, do you?" She didn't wait for an answer. "It must be my fault. I should have remarried sooner. He needed a father figure in his life, someone to show him a healthy relationship."

"Mmhm," I muttered between bites. Ryan owed me so big time.

"Promise me you'll be careful about who you lose your heart to, Bethany. No more Todds. It's so important to pick the right person."

After fifteen minutes, she let me hang up. Fifteen minutes protecting her from Ryan's problems and my broken heart. I wondered what Carter was doing as I took another fun size candy bar out of the jar.

CHAPTER 24

Co-workers bombarded me when I showed up to work Monday, all wanting the gooey details. Luckily, I'd come up with a plan.

"I'm sorry, I signed a confidentiality agreement. I can't say anything yet."

This worked on everyone except my boss, Mr. Langley. He listened to me give my automatic response in the hallway and then motioned me over with a grim look. "Bethany, I'd like to see you in my office."

He closed the door behind us and waited for me to sit down.

"Why are you here?"

Oh, no. Did he not see my email?

"You asked for a month off. It's only been two weeks. That's not enough time to fall in love."

So everyone keeps telling me. "I did my best, Mr. Langley, but six of us got eliminated in one night, leaving only two couples. The show is making the last two couples stay the final two weeks. I don't think the voting worked out the way the director thought it would."

Mr. Langley frowned. "What kind of an idiot lets that happen?"

I pictured Dave's sweatpants and greasy hair and hid a smile.

"Oh well. If you're ready to dive back in, here's what I need from you. Jeffy is supposed to do an endorsement for an orthopedic pillow, but we sent the company his tape and they hate it. I need you to work with that clown and make his endorsement sound genuine. I'd fire him, except listeners like his celebrity impersonations. Tell him he's not allowed to sound like a Muppet in this ad. Next, I need you to shorten up a Honda dealership commercial. We'll need a thirty second ad and a fifteen second clip..."

I started making notes as a feeling of personal satisfaction came over me. Mr. Langley wasn't keeping me because I might get fifteen minutes of fame, he was keeping me because I was good at my job. Why had I doubted that? I'd let Todd belittle me for too long, and it was time to let it go. I was needed here, I did good work and it paid the bills.

After leaving Mr. Langley's office with my to-do list, I went to my desk and put my headphones on so I could listen to Jeffy's endorsement. It was as bad as Mr. Langley said. Jeffy was still on the air, so I checked the website for the pillow and read up on it.

I knew what would happen when I mentioned it to Jeffy. He'd ask if we could talk about it over lunch at a nearby restaurant. He'd insist I call him Jeff and try to smooth down his wiry hair. Since he had to be in every morning at 4:30 a.m. to get on the air by 5:00, he couldn't fulfill his dream of being a ladies man. He'd tell me how lonely he was at night, while staring at me with hungry eyes. I was starting to think he screwed up his marketing bits on purpose. And if that were true, it was time to squelch the lunches.

***

Jeffy sauntered over to my desk after his midmorning meeting and pulled up a chair. "Bethany, glad to have you back. About this pillow. I left it at home and I was thinking we could head over to my apartment during lunch."

He nudged me in the shoulder. "Try it out, you may," he croaked out in a Yoda voice.

Ignoring and avoiding his advances had not been working. If anything, it was making it worse. My mind flitted to Carter. *I know you're not happy about this. So let's be brutally honest with each other.*

"Jeffy, let me be honest. I'm not interested in you. Not even a little bit. We're co-workers and I'm trying to help you keep your job. If you don't bring in revenue for the station, Mr. Langley will fire you. Companies should be begging you to endorse their products. But instead, you're doing endorsements maybe once a month for low-revenue products like this pillow."

Jeffy scooted his chair back. "Enough said. I was only trying to be nice. You went on a reality show to find a guy and came back early. I'm assuming you didn't find what you were looking for and could use a little attention."

"I don't need your attention, Jeffy. I'm fine."

Dang it, now I was not fine. I missed Carter—fiercely.

"Well if you change your mind…"

I dropped my head on my desk and sighed. "I'm not going to change my mind. I couldn't even have a fling with a guy I'm desperately in love with."

Okay, maybe I shouldn't have been *that* brutally honest.

"Who's this guy?" Patty asked excitedly.

I looked up and saw her leaning against my desk. "No one. I was speaking hypothetically."

Jeffy and Patty exchanged looks. They didn't believe me for a second.

"Can we talk about this when I interview you on the air?" Jeffy asked.

No! "This has nothing to do with the reality show."

Jeffy leaned in, "You're a terrible liar. Some insanely handsome guy tried to seduce you, you turned him down, and then he sent you home. That's why you have sad eyes and why I don't have a chance. Every night you go to bed thinking, 'if only.' But I'd never treat you like that."

Patty stared at me with sympathy. "Men are pigs."

I gritted my teeth. It wouldn't matter if I denied it. That's how I'd made it sound and that's usually how these shows went. "Think whatever you want. Just keep your crazy theories off the air. I thought Sherry was interviewing me. You're supposed to play sidekick. Add humorous comments and stuff."

Jeffy grinned. "Sherry's moving to hard rock and I'm getting a side kick. Sherry and Jeffy in the morning never sounded right anyway."

There was no use worrying about it. Jeffy could be gone by then, too. DJ's came and went like Henry VIII's wives. In the meantime, I needed to get our conversation back on track. "Jeffy, go get your pillow at lunch and bring it back here. We've got work to do."

Ryan burst through the front door while I was making dinner, smiling like the world belonged to him.

"She called me."

He sat down on a kitchen chair and peeled off his sweaty baseball cap.

"Yuck, don't put that on the table. There's a hook right over there."

He plopped his hat on the wall and then came over to investigate. "Ooh, spaghetti. Jasmine wants to meet for dinner so save me some leftovers. I'll take them to work tomorrow. If I'm still here."

I was happy for him, but his optimism was scaring me. "Slow down and tell me what she said."

Ryan sat back down at the table and propped his feet up on a chair. "She misses me and wants me to come home."

When he didn't continue I turned around and looked at him. "Did she say anything about what's-his-name? The bridesman?"

Ryan's eyebrows furrowed. "No. I didn't want to get right into another fight when she'd just called me. But I told her we should talk everything out before I came home. That's why we're going to dinner."

I nodded. "That's good."

Ryan eyed me. "You're not telling me what you really think."

What I thought was that Jasmine would wear something slinky to dinner and bat her eyes and Ryan would cave so they could go back to having everything her way, on her terms. But I wasn't going to say that.

"I think it's a good idea to talk. But make sure that's all you do until you work this out."

Ryan picked up a heating pad from the table and tossed it at me. "I can't have this conversation with my sister. I'm going to go shower and get ready. Don't wait up."

So now I had the evening to myself with too much spaghetti. I ate and then packaged up the leftovers as Ryan hurried out the door, dripping in cologne.

And then, because there was no one there to stop me, I looked up Carter on social media like a stalker and stared at his picture. He didn't get on Facebook much. His last post was a photo of him in the snow with his little sister. He needed to tighten his profile security before the show aired. But I couldn't tell him that, because I'd promised myself I'd move on.

I snapped my computer shut and collapsed on my pillow. There was no way I could stay like this, moping around and thinking about him. I forced myself off the bed and headed for the closet to change into workout clothes. It was time to dust off my gym membership.

***

Early the next morning, I woke up to sounds in the spare bedroom. Ryan was home, finally. I peeked my head in the doorway and raised an eyebrow.

"I don't want to hear it."

"I'm not Mom, Ryan. I'm not going to lecture you."

He gave me a sheepish look and continued packing. I went in to make him breakfast and we sat together and talked about NFL football teams while we ate. My knowledge of the sport could maybe fill up an index card, but I did my best. We both had topics we wanted to avoid.

Patty tried every way possible to get me to spill my guts at work. But I was not about to slip up again. After Jeffy's comment about my 'sad eyes,' I tried much harder to rein in thoughts about Carter, at least at work. The last thing I wanted was to add more fuel to the gossip fire at our radio station. People that talk for a living eat up gossip like a favorite dessert.

I threw myself into concert ticket giveaways, commercials, community fundraisers, sponsorships for the traffic reports and anything else Mr. Langley needed done. At first, he treated me strangely when I kept coming into his office for more work, but he wasn't about to tell me to stop. My phone buzzed as I was cleaning up my desk to leave for the day.

"Bethany Parks?"

"That's me."

"This is The Phoenix Flower Shop. We're at your home with a delivery for you. Is there a convenient time to come back?"

Someone sent me flowers? "Oh, I'm still at work. But I'm almost done."

"We could deliver it to your workplace if that's more

convenient."

"No, no. I'm leaving in a minute. You can put it on the porch."

"Are you sure?"

"Yes."

I gathered up my things and headed to my car. Darn, I hadn't even asked who the flowers were from. Although it was kind of nice to wonder about it on the drive home. Maybe it was a thank you bouquet from Ryan. If they were from Jeffy, we'd have to have another talk about work boundaries. For both our sakes, I was trying to leave HR out of this.

A goofy grin snuck across my face as I pulled into the driveway and saw the gorgeous long-stem red roses. *Please don't be from Todd.* I ran across the front lawn and plucked the card off the vase.

We'll always be friends.
- Carter

What? I sank onto the front step and stared at the card, hoping the words would change before my eyes. How could something so romantic come with a message like that? And what did he mean? Was he going to marry Holly? Even for a pessimist like me, it still came as a total shock and I didn't want to believe it. Dang it, I'd tried to protect my heart from something like this and it didn't help. Not even a little bit. I couldn't imagine feeling worse than I did now.

I tucked my phone against my ear after dialing Katelyn and unlocked my door. Although tempted to leave the flowers outside, I reluctantly picked up the vase and put them on the counter.

"Can you come over? I know you probably can't—" I started crying and couldn't finish.

"Yes, we'll be right over. And by 'we' I mean me and Doug Jr. I'll keep my sarcastic husband at home. Hang on."

I grabbed up a rag and started wiping down the cupboards. *Focus on dust. Don't think yet.* When I'd reached the end of the cupboards, I got out a broom and swept the kitchen.

"I brought cinnamon rolls," Katelyn sang as she walked in with Doug Jr. She stopped at the sight of the flowers and then took in my tear-streaked face. "I don't understand."

"Me either."

"Who sent them?"

"The guy from the show."

"Mr. I-Can't-Fly?"

She reached out and read the card before dropping it on the floor. "That's horrible."

"I know." But even as she said that, my mind started rebelling against the thought. Carter was never cruel, even when he was balancing his feelings for me with his obligation to Holly. And how did he send the roses? He didn't have his phone...or my address. Did Dave put him up to this?

"If he's picking the other girl, he's an idiot." Katelyn came over to give me a hug and Doug Jr. began to fuss.

I stroked his head. "He's bigger already. Look at those cheeks."

Katelyn smiled down at her baby and started telling me what a good eater he was. Then she glanced up and cocked her head. "Wait. Don't do that. I know you think you don't want to talk about this guy, but you called me over here because you do."

So I purged, starting with meeting Carter and how he told me about Todd's interview. I described everything I'd ever noticed about him and all the reasons I couldn't get him out of my head. Then I described Holly, all her sides, from crazy and clingy, to devious and focused.

"He asked for your number and you didn't give it to him?"

"Yes, but—"

"And now he's sent flowers and you're crying about it? I'm changing my vote. I think the flowers are a good sign. Maybe the message came out wrong. I mean, look at these. They're gorgeous."

"But what about Dave? What about Holly?"

"We're totally overthinking this. Enjoy the flowers and give it time. If you never hear from him again, then I guess it meant what we first thought."

"I guess," I answered, moodily.

"Hey, let's look up his music." Katelyn searched on her phone until she found it and I reluctantly leaned over to listen to a sample song with her.

Carter had never sung to me on the show, but he was a choir teacher so I assumed he'd sing well. What I didn't expect was how it would make me feel. His voice was unmistakable and without affectation, just a sincere, straightforward style, like he was sitting right next to me at the piano. A terrible homesickness for him rose up and I shook my head. "I can't listen to it."

"Why?" Katelyn asked. "His sister is adorable. I love her voice." She glanced up at me and her smile dropped. "I'm so sorry. What can I do for you?"

I held out my arms. "Let me hold Mr. Chubby for a while. And let's talk about something else."

So we discussed Doug's aversion to changing diapers while I rubbed my cheek against Doug Jr.'s warm fuzzy head.

After Katelyn left, I put the roses on a shelf in the pantry and ate a cinnamon roll. It tasted like disappointment.

CHAPTER 25

My boss called me into his office the next morning, looking excited. "I heard from your show."

"You did?" I plopped in the chair across from his desk.

"Yes. NBC sold *Real Love* to The Reality Network. Not super excited about that. But, it's getting on TV, soon. The Reality Network is using it as a last minute replacement. Some poor guy dropped dead of a heart attack on their gladiator show so they needed something immediately to finish off the summer season. *Real Love* came at the perfect time."

"But they haven't even finished filming." Dave was probably devastated he wouldn't be on NBC. I felt a little guilty for the relief that washed over me, knowing I'd be hidden on a small cable channel. And how terrible that the cause of it had to do with someone's death.

Mr. Langley shrugged. "I don't know. Sounds like the big wigs didn't like how things were going. Arc shows are tricky. With no set script and no exact outcome, it's hard to predict if you have a winner on your hands until the end. But back to business. They sent us an audio clip and said to start using it immediately. Here's a list of things you're not allowed to talk about until after an episode airs."

I took the paper and skimmed down the page. Basically, I couldn't talk about outcomes at all, except in vague, preapproved ways, like saying how happy I was with how everything turned out. From the looks of it, I couldn't tell anyone it hadn't turned out how I'd wanted, until America saw it for themselves. Mr. Langley gave me a minute to look it over before continuing.

"You're going on air at the top of next hour. Don't worry, it will only be to introduce yourself after they play the promo. We'll have a full meeting about this as soon as we get an exact air date for the premier."

I nodded, my insides tossing like clothes in a dryer. Why didn't I get a call first? Typical Dave.

"Oh, and plan on checking all the entertainment magazines as soon as the new issues come out, See if they have any articles about your show. We'll go over them on the air with Sherry and Jeffy."

At least this would happen while Sherry was still here. Jeffy would be disappointed not to lead the interviews.

My mind turned to the roses sitting in my dark pantry. Soon everyone would be asking me about my relationship with Carter. Maybe they could analyze it with me and come up with some answers. I wasn't getting any. I shuffled out of Mr. Langley's office, leaving him with his excitement and plans. My privacy vacation was over.

***

"This is Sherry, your morning goddess, and we're back with a very special guest. Isn't that right Jeffy?"

"That's right, Sherry. Bethany Parks works in advertising here on KYLM Country Radio, but in her other life she's breaking hearts on *Real Love*, the new dating reality show coming soon to The Reality Network."

"Say hi, Bethany." Sherry nodded at me and curled her fingers up around her mouth, reminding me to smile. Even a fake one helped energize the voice.

I thought of Tyson and plastered on a smile. "Hi KYLM listeners. There's a lot I can't tell you, but I am allowed to say I auditioned for this reality show back in January after I broke up with my boyfriend, Todd. And then I got on the show and Todd was there, along with the exes of the other women with me."

Sherry laughed. "Sounds like we'll enjoy watching your pain. Are you fully recovered after all that dating drama?"

"I'm getting back to normal."

Jeffy winked at me. "Well don't keep us waiting, Sherry. Play the promo."

"I sure will, right after a word from our sponsors. Don't go anywhere." Sherry hit the mute button, leaned back in her chair and took off her headphones. "Good job, Bethany. I'm going to do a quick reintroduction after the break and then we'll play it and you can go."

The only good thing about this, besides the fact that we were almost done, was Sherry. She'd been on radio forever and was as professional as they came. She couldn't care less about gossip, unless the job required it. She sipped her gigantic Diet Coke and didn't say another word until we were back from commercials.

"And we're back with Bethany Parks. She works in advertising here on KYLM, but she's also a contestant on the upcoming Reality Network show, *Real Love*. We have an exclusive, first promo for all you listeners. Bethany, you've never heard this before, correct?"

"Never heard it."

"Play the tape, you will," Jeffy croaked.

Peppy music started and then a movie voice broke out with, "What if dating on TV was just like dating at home? Our fifteen contestants thought they were headed for luxury and roses, but we put them in bargain clothes, gave them chores, sent them on realistic dates, and to be even more authentic, added their exes into the mix." The tape cut to Jada's voice. "I'm not over my ex. If any of you make a move on him, I'll cut you." Then back to movie voice. "Stay tuned America. Real people, real exes, *Real Love*. Coming soon to The Reality Network."

Sherry turned to me. "So what do you think, Bethany? Does that sound like an accurate description of your show?"

I leaned into the microphone. "Unfortunately, yes."

***

After making it through the interview and dealing with all the Facebook and Twitter comments from interested listeners, I was so ready for quitting time. Traffic crawled on the way home and my brain was tired of radio, so I kept it off.

I raced up my front walkway and locked the front door behind me, before stripping down to my underwear and making myself a sandwich.

It made me giggle to realize Tyson and I had something in common. At the end of a stressful day, nothing made me feel better.

I hadn't contacted Tyson since the show, needing some space from everything, even him, but I also wanted to find out what was going on. So I texted him.

You hear about the show being sold?

Tyson answered a few minutes later. **Yep. U ready for this?**

I frowned. **No, but you know that. Kinda hoped it would get cancelled. After they pay us, of course.**

Don't worry. Dave says check's in the mail

So Dave had been calling people. **You talked to him?**

My phone rang with a call from Tyson. I guess his answer wouldn't fit in a text message.

"What are you wearing?" Tyson asked in a silky voice.

I looked down at my cream colored bra and laughed. "Sweats. Green ones with frogs on them."

"Sounds hot. Dave called me yesterday. He said he was trying to book TV interviews for me and I should do the same. He didn't ask you to do that?"

"He hasn't called me."

"He probably assumed you'd tell him no. It's not in our contract so he can't make us." Tyson laughed. "But he knows I'll do anything for attention."

"In that case, he should call Holly."

"I'm sure he has." Tyson got quiet. "Hey, has Carter called you?"

"How would he call? He's still on the show."

"Of course," Tyson answered quickly. "Forgot about that. Babe, I gotta go. Send me some flirty texts occasionally, okay?"

Tyson hung up and I stared at my phone, trying to figure out what that all meant. But I didn't get time to dwell on it because someone was pounding on my front door and I was sitting at the kitchen table in my bra and underwear. After throwing on a pair of pants and a T-shirt, I ran to the door and looked through the peephole. Ryan. And Jasmine. They were both frowning.

I steeled myself for whatever this was and opened the door. "Hi guys."

Ryan came inside and glanced back at Jasmine. She rolled her eyes and stepped in, looking like she'd rather be anywhere else.

"Jasmine thinks marriage counseling is too expensive, but I said we needed to talk to someone. Since you already know what's going on, I was hoping we could talk to you."

He pulled out a chair for Jasmine and she sat down and stared at me. "Ryan thinks you're going to change my mind."

I doubt it. Why did everything always meet my expectations? The upside to being a pessimist was that good news would take me by surprise. But I hadn't gotten good news about Carter and clearly I'd been right about Ryan and Jasmine. She hadn't changed at all. Right now, I wanted nothing more than to be wrong about something.

Ryan and Jasmine were looking at me expectantly, so I turned my focus back to them. Couldn't they at least have called and run the idea by me first? No, I would have talked him out of it.

"What's going on?"

Ryan looked at Jasmine, hoping she'd speak first. But her face made it clear that wasn't going to happen. "She promised me she'd spend less time with Edward, but this morning I woke up and she was on her phone. It was 4:30 a.m. She won't let me look at her text messages."

Time for all my wisdom. All my counseling skills from years of successful relationships. As if. I was so not cut out for this. "You were texting Edward?" I asked Jasmine.

Her mouth turned pouty. "It doesn't matter. We're only friends. He needed to talk."

"Then why can't I see the messages?" Ryan pleaded.

"Because you should trust me. I can't stay in a marriage where I feel like I'm being spied on."

"I wouldn't ask if you weren't being sneaky. Are you saying you have nothing to hide?"

The two of them went back and forth while I sat back and felt a headache coming on. They needed therapy, bad. I got up to make myself a cup of tea.

Jasmine saw the box of chamomile tea in my hands. "Oh, I'd love a cup."

I blinked back at her and made a decision. "I've heard enough. Ryan, I love you, but I'm not a therapist. If you need a place to stay, the spare bedroom is yours."

Jasmine gaped at me. "You said you wanted to help."

"Actually, I never said that. I let you guys in. If you want me to make you some tea, stop arguing with my brother. You're giving me a headache."

She closed her mouth and stared down at her hands. "Okay."

They sat in silence while I puttered around making the tea, and some ramen noodle soup for Ryan. He could eat the stuff for breakfast, lunch and dinner.

"You know I love you," Jasmine finally said, looking at Ryan.

He stared straight ahead, as if he hadn't heard her.

Her face dropped and she looked over to me for support.

"The feeling is great, but you need to show it. True love is doing what's best for the two of you, not just what's best for you." I hoped that was the right thing for me to say.

The kitchen clock ticked and Ryan sipped his soup. I didn't know if all this silence was a good thing or not, but it had to be better than arguing.

"Fine, I'll delete his number and tell him we can't be friends anymore." She said it so quietly we almost didn't hear her.

"Don't do me any favors," Ryan muttered. I wanted to punch him, but I understood his hurt. She made it sound like that concession was her whole world.

She opened her mouth to argue, but I put my hand out and she stopped. More silence. My phone rang. I didn't recognize the number and rejected the call. I looked up and saw Ryan reach out and take Jasmine's hand.

"Edward helped me through a bad breakup in college. I feel…I felt like I owed him. But he's been saying things he shouldn't say. I don't say them back, and I haven't done anything…physical, but I'm sorry. I should have ended things a long time ago. Last night he…" She glanced at me and stopped talking.

There were things needed to be said that were not for my ears. "You two go home and talk."

They nodded and got up, pushing in their chairs. I shut the door behind them and let out a great sigh. What a day. It was time for my green frog sweats. I did the dishes, brushed my teeth and climbed into bed with a book I knew would put me to sleep in no time at all. Just as I was drifting off, my phone rang again. It was the same number as before. Probably Dave, and I didn't want to talk to him. After having Ryan and Jasmine over, I didn't want to talk to anyone. I waited for the voicemail notification and then checked the message.

"Hi, Bethany. It's Carter."

Breathe, woman, just breathe.

CHAPTER 26

Call me? How could his message be so casual? Because what I heard in those two words was, *I've decided money is more important than true love, but hey, I like closure.*

At first I thought I'd go to sleep and let him stew overnight, but on hearing his message, my body decided I'd never be sleepy ever again. Every few minutes, I'd stop drumming on the bed and check my phone again for the time. And then I'd put the phone back and try to figure out what was going on inside Carter's head. He was supposed to have another week on the show. Was he calling from there?

I couldn't take it anymore and hit the call back button. One ring. Two. Three.

"Hi, Bethany."

"I don't want to talk to you." *Which is why I called, to not talk to you.* Being mad and nervous at the same time did not make me logical.

"I figured that. You wouldn't give me your number. But you gave it to Tyson. He says hi." There was humor in his voice, but a bit of hurt, too. I had to remind myself he was the one that dumped me with flowers.

"I got your flowers."

"I'm so glad. Trusting Dave to send them was not ideal." He laughed nervously.

Part of me wanted to hang up right then. But hearing his voice took me back to staying in our apartment together. Our little slice on non-reality heaven. What happened to us? What did Holly do to him?

The silence stretched out. A polite response would be to comment on the beauty of the roses or to thank him, but I did neither. And I wouldn't until he explained himself.

"Bethany, I'm going to be honest with you and I hope you'll be honest with me. I'm clueless around women usually, but around you I might as well slide back into the primordial ooze. What happened? I know you think I know. But trust me, I have no idea what you're mad about. Please, please tell me."

"The message you sent with the roses. Does that mean you and Holly won the engagement ring and modeling contract?" I hated admitting my fear out loud.

"No. No. I told Dave to send you roses. He owed us each a favor and that's what I picked. I should have known he'd screw it up. What did the card say? I'm afraid to ask."

The message wasn't from Carter. Tears blurred my eyes and I felt like an idiot for believing otherwise. "It said, 'We'll always be friends.' I thought that meant you were saying goodbye."

"I'm going to slug Dave if I ever see him again, although I'm hoping I never do. Bethany, why would you think I'd marry Holly? She's a friend. That's it."

"I know that." Annoyance crept up, but I pushed it back down. I'd punished Carter enough for one conversation. "But I figured Holly would talk you into a fake engagement so you could get the money. Maybe even sell the $50,000 ring in a few years, you know, to pay off your sister's medical bills."

"I wouldn't do that, and the $50,000 ring got downgraded to a $15,000 ring anyway. When NBC told Dave they'd sold the show to The Reality Network, a lot of crap hit the fan. Dave had to sweet talk the jeweler to even stay on board. The last week of filming got axed. He had two days left to wrap up the show and end with a bang. He ordered Marco and me to propose. Marco agreed, I refused. Jada threw a tantrum about the ring downgrade and about being on a show that nobody would ever see. That's when we got our favors from Dave. The next day, Marco and Jada got engaged and Holly proposed to me and I turned her down. Lots of fake crying all around. And that was a wrap."

"You're home then?"

"Yep. Holly was recovering from food poisoning so I had to fly without her. After the crew realized I was sweaty and nervous because I hate flying and not because I had a bomb, they assigned a nice flight attendant to hold my hand and gave me a set of wings from the captain."

"Wow, you lucky boy." I laughed.

"It's so good to hear you laugh. I miss you."

"I miss you, too." I wanted to reach through the phone and kiss him, but at the same time, I hated that the phone call had turned sentimental. It only reminded me we had no way to remedy the situation. "Carter, I don't want a long distance relationship."

"I know," he quickly responded. "I shouldn't have said anything mushy. You are so predictable."

"I am not." Now I wanted to pinch him.

"You are too. Stop hyperventilating and tell me about your day."

So I told him about work and Katelyn's new baby. When I got to Ryan and Jasmine, I felt a twinge of discomfort telling him about Jasmine's emotional affair. It didn't make sense for me to compare it to Carter and Holly. Even though it sounded like Carter and Holly were still friends, and it still bothered me, Carter and I weren't married or even boyfriend/girlfriend. I wasn't even sure I could define us if someone asked.

***

"When someone can't stop smiling and yawning, I know they've got a good story to tell." Patty grinned down at me as she dropped a file on my desk.

If I thought for one second Patty was being friendly and not digging for gossip, I might divulge. But, then again, probably not. I hadn't even called Katelyn to tell her about Carter's phone call. He was my happy secret, and if I told Katelyn we'd end up analyzing things. I did enough of that on my own.

My phone buzzed, alerting me to a text message, but I made myself wait until Patty was safely back at her desk before looking at it.

You as tired as I am?

Yep, I need a nap. Maybe at lunch.

Holly pounded on my door at 8. She wanted to make sure I was alive since I hadn't called her yet. She's worse than my

mother.

I thought of a few choice texts to answer that, but I refrained. *Be mature.* **What are you doing today?**

Mowing lawns, then selling snow cones at the park.

Carter had told me about all the odd jobs he did in the summer when he wasn't teaching. He'd bought a food trailer a few years ago and added commercial appliances when he could afford it. In the summer he sold pop, chips, soft serve ice cream and snow cones. During Christmas break he sold cookies, coffee and hot chocolate. We'd kept things light up until then. I hadn't been prepared for how he ended the conversation. *"Bethany, I work as hard as I can every day, squirreling away money. But what I really want is a reason for all of it. Someone to come home to."*

My response? Nothing. I told him I'd talk to him tomorrow. That was the limit of my commitment. I'd let him call me again. I had trust issues, maybe from Todd, maybe because of the show and Holly, maybe from my pessimism. They were all tied together so tightly I couldn't see the difference anymore.

But Carter had faith in me, in us, and I loved that about him. I'd told him how sorry I was for not being willing to give things a try. I'd been a quitter, and while I was still hesitant, I wanted to see where things would go. I owed it to myself and to him.

My daily task list was piling up, so I texted Carter to let him know I had to go, put my phone away and got to work. After all, if Mr. Langley got an itch to put me on the radio again today, I'd better have all this done first.

I checked my phone again before heading off to lunch. One recent text from Tyson: **How's Carter?**

I'll punch you. Of course Tyson would check in. Mr. Matchmaker.

That good, huh. I can't believe you didn't give him your number when he asked for it. That's cold.

Ouch. I knew my lame apology would never be enough, even though Carter had assured me it was. Leave it to Tyson to lay it all out and make me face my stupidity.

You still there? Did I hurt your feelings?

I rolled my eyes. **I'm wounded, but I'll recover.**

It was my turn at the drive-thru window, so I put my phone down, got my food and paid. I hated eating in my car, but with the options of eating alone inside or going back to the dingy breakroom at the radio station, it was my best option.

Mom called two bites into my burger. Darn it. She knew when my lunch break began and ended and expected me to answer.

"Hi Mom."

"Hi sweetie. I know it's last minute, but I'd love it if you could come for dinner tonight. I already called Ryan and Jasmine and they're coming."

My brain fumbled over possible excuses, but to my mother a pause meant confirmation.

"Great! I'll see you at six o'clock. Wear something nice. Oh, and bring a green salad."

She hung up and I rested my forehead against the steering wheel. *But mom, I have plans. I'm going to talk on the phone with my…with the guy I love and who might love me, but we haven't said it yet. It's complicated.*

***

Mom's admonition to dress up had me worried. Why did I have to wear something nice? Clutching my salad bowl, I walked up to the front door and gave a light knock before letting myself in. Ryan met me in the foyer and took the bowl from me. "I'm so sorry."

"Why are you sorry?" I could hear Jasmine in the kitchen talking to Mom, and then my stepdad's booming laugh.

"Mom brought you a date."

Heck no. I turned around and reached for the doorknob, but Mom had already come down the hall and spotted me.

"Bethany, come meet Steve's work friend. I've already introduced him to Ryan and Jasmine." She said it loud enough to be heard in the other room, making it awkward for me if I were to leave now. I reluctantly pulled my hand off the door and followed her down the hall, elbowing Ryan before we entered the dining room.

"A warning text would have been nice."

Ryan grinned at me. "I'll try not to enjoy this too much."

I caught Jasmine's look of sympathy before my eyes lighted on Mom's guest.

"This is Jonas. He's a dentist at Steve's practice." Jonas reached out a soft hand and I shook it, trying not to stare at the tuft of hair in the middle of his chin. Ryan had a soul patch in high school and

I threatened to hold him down and shave it off on a regular basis. This guy was pushing forty and had no excuse for his stringy little hair fad. Plus, as a dentist, he'd be wagging that thing in patients' faces. Not mine, thank you very much.

"Nice to meet you, Jonas." His face was handsome, even with his hair accessory and I had to admit, he wasn't the worst specimen Mom had thrown at me over the years. She was getting bolder. Usually Mom called and talked my ear off about someone she thought might be perfect for me. A surprise blind date was a new low.

Jonas met my gaze and then his eyes drifted down. Even though my neckline was fine, I felt the need to tug at it under Jonas's inspection.

My stepdad, Steve, had the decency to look a bit uncomfortable. "Jonas, how did Mrs. Henderson's crowns go this morning?"

Jonas tore his eyes away from me and cleared his throat. "It went well. I gave her a follow up call right before I came and she's fine."

"Oh, Steve. Talk shop tomorrow." Mom winked at me and placed the roasted chicken on the table before sitting down between Steve and Jonas.

"Can I help you get anything else from the kitchen?" I asked, giving her a pointed look.

"It's all here, dear. I was telling Jonas before we came that you recently went on a reality dating show."

Jonas nodded at me as he filled his plate with salad. "That's brave of you. It's not the sort of way I'd like to meet someone, but interesting." He nodded some more, as if trying to make it less of a dig.

"Yes. I'm relieved she didn't find anyone." Mom added. "It's much better to date someone close to home and get to know them the old fashioned way. Like Ryan and Jasmine did."

Ryan took a long drink from his cup as all eyes turned to him. "Yep. We're so happy. Aren't we Jaz?"

Jasmine plastered on a smile and then asked Steve if he'd pass the potatoes.

"So, Jonas. Tell us a little about yourself." Mom's eyes shined in anticipation. "Besides being an amazing dentist, what do you like to do?"

Jonas squirmed in his chair and finished chewing his last bite.

He doesn't want to be here either.

"I like to oil paint. I have a studio set up in my apartment and on the weekends that's what I do to relax."

"How nice. Have you sold any paintings?"

I cringed. He was a dentist, not a famous artist. *Knock it off, Mom.*

"Mom, he said he paints to destress. Not to make money."

"Actually several galleries carry my work. My mother always said it was vulgar to talk about money, but I will say, it's been a lucrative hobby." He chuckled and Mom joined him.

Any sympathy I'd felt for him vaporized, now that he was giving off a Todd vibe. The last thing I needed was another guy who always had to feel superior.

I ate as fast as possible and tried not to make eye contact with Mom as she chattered on. But it wasn't fast enough.

"Bethany, I'm so glad you and Jonas get to meet each other. Jonas recently broke up with someone, too. And even just meeting a new friend is nice. Bethany's best friend recently had a baby, so she doesn't have as much time for Bethany these days."

It amazed me that someone so obtuse could also be so observant. Yes, I'd let other friendships dwindle in the past few years, especially after I started dating Todd. Yes, Katelyn was moving on to a new era in her life. But I was way too old to put up with this. I took a deep breath and stood.

"Mom, I love you, but I'm going to leave now. I'll get my salad bowl from you later. Jonas, nice to meet you. Good to see you Steve. Ryan, Jasmine, take care of each other."

I grabbed my purse off the hook in the foyer and closed the door quietly behind me before running to my car. With the adrenaline pumping through me, I dialed Carter.

"Bethany, can you hold on a min—"

"Carter, I love you. And I'm saying it now because this bravery thing is going to wear off any minute. I have no idea what to do about it, but I love you."

Carter breathed heavily into the phone and then I heard what I never wanted to hear after declaring how I felt to him: Holly's voice in the background, saying "just listen to me." And then Carter hung up the phone.

CHAPTER 27

Hot tears coursed down my face as I pulled into my driveway. I wiped them away, trying desperately to hang onto my dignity. If this was the price of being brave, then I could handle it. Because the alternative was sitting through excruciating double dates with my parents.

Carter called as I was unlocking my door and I let it go to voicemail. The stress from the evening made me feel stiff all over and I went to take a shower, staying in until the hot water ran out. After combing out my hair, pulling my green frog sweats out of the dryer, and climbing under the covers, I gave into the temptation to check my phone again.

There were several text messages like **Please let me explain** and **I love you.** Was there anything worse than hearing 'I love you' for the first time during an apology? I would not be swayed so easily. And I wouldn't let him try. Not tonight, anyway. After putting my phone on silent, I turned on the TV and stared at it mindlessly for a few hours before drifting off to a restless sleep. *Why didn't he ever stand up to Holly?*

My eyes felt raw and my heart hurt when I woke the next morning and everything came flooding back. I didn't even look at my phone, just shoved it in my bag as I headed out to work.

Of course Mr. Langley wanted me on the radio immediately. Because what goes best with a bad mood and inner turmoil? Being put on the spot.

Jeffy patted me on the back when I walked into the studio and I resisted the urge to grab his hand and twist. It wasn't his fault my love life was a mess. I took the set of headphones from him and gave him what I hoped was a genuine smile as we sat down with Sherry. She mouthed, "twenty seconds."

After the commercial break, Sherry explained to our listeners that The Reality Network had announced a premier date for *Real Love* and then replayed the promo clip from last time. Every few seconds Jeffy would bellow like Chewbacca or add a comment in a Kermit the Frog voice.

Sherry asked listeners to call in with their questions for me and then started a song so they could screen the calls.

"You think anyone will call in with a real question?" I knew people had starting asking about the show on our Facebook page, but the thought of being questioned live was a bit unnerving.

"Don't worry. We have a ten second delay if anyone goes off the rails. You get ready to be friendly and vague. Don't reveal any cliffhangers, am I right?" She laughed and I grimaced.

No pressure.

The song ended and Sherry introduced me for anyone newly tuning in. Then she opened up line one.

"Yes, hi, I was wondering how many contestants there are. Like is it a bunch of women fighting over a guy or a bunch of guys fighting over you?"

An easy one. "The first episode has eight guys and seven women. It's unlike anything you'll have seen before."

Sherry nodded her approval and went to caller two.

"I heard you the other day and I was wondering if you could tell me what it was like having exes on there. Did couples get back together? Did you get back together with your ex?"

This would be easy, too. I couldn't answer any of that. "Well, there was definitely fighting and jealousy, but I can't say who ended up together. You'll have to watch and find out."

Mr. Langley was standing against the door and he grinned at me and gave me a thumbs up.

"Okay, we'll take one more call and then stay with us, because up next is fifty minutes of the best country music in Arizona." Sherry hit the button for caller three.

"Hi Bethany."

Carter? I let out a squeak and then covered my mouth with my hands.

"I was wondering if there was a crazy girl on *Real Love*. You know, the one that fools the guy and sabotages the other relationships. I saw that once on a show, where she grabbed a phone out of a guy's hand, and it was a really important phone call. And then he had to make her leave before he could try to call back."

All eyes turned to me and I had to remind myself that I had to finish this, then freak out. Not the other way around.

"Well, random caller. We weren't allowed to have phones. But there was a girl like that. Seems like there always is. It makes good TV, after all."

Sherry introduced the newest country song and then took off her headphones. "You did great, Bethany." She shook my hand and then left for a bathroom break.

I nodded and smiled at everyone as my mind whirled. The booth felt like it was closing in on me and I couldn't focus on anything. I had to get out of there. Mr. Langley said something about an assignment and I took whatever he handed me and ran to my desk. *Carter, why do you have to turn my life upside down and inside out?*

Our relationship had been far from normal and the roller coaster was exhausting. I couldn't believe he'd gone so far as to call in to get me to talk to him. It showed me he was willing to fight for me, but would it be enough to make things work between us? I wasn't sure.

$$***$$

There were flowers on my front porch again when I got home. Purple tulips this time. The card said, 'All my love, Carter.' I smiled and put them on the counter, touching each one before going in the pantry and getting out the roses. The urge to call Carter was killing me, but I needed time to figure out exactly what I wanted to say. So I headed out for a run to clear my head. By the time I'd jogged back to my driveway thirty minutes later, I'd come to some conclusions. And I wasn't even ashamed that Ryan and Jasmine's situation helped me figure it out.

I loved Carter. He was so easy to fall for and I loved everything about him—except for the Holly infestation. He could explain all he wanted to, but I'd have to say goodbye and let him go if he was still going to be friends with her, even casually. And worst of all, I couldn't tell him that. Any of it. He'd have to choose it on his own. Because that was the kind of love I wanted. The kind where I put him first and he put me first and we didn't have to beg each other to do it. And then…the scariest part was considering a time when I might have to tell my mom I was moving to Minot, North Dakota. Maybe I'd tell her after I did it, this theoretical move after Carter and I worked everything out. A pessimist can dream, sometimes. She just worries about all the ways the dream can go wrong.

I considered listening to the four messages Carter had left me, but decided I wanted to hear it from him. So I sat down at the kitchen table and dialed him.

"Bethany! Don't hang up. Please don't hang up. I'm sorry I called your radio station. That was a little stalkerish. But I didn't sleep at all and then I remembered you saying they'd put you on the radio and probably would again so I listened over the internet all morning hoping to hear you. That Jeffy guy is really annoying."

"Yes, he is. But he's also sweet."

"You did great on the radio today."

"Carter, save the compliments for after your explanation. What happened with Holly?"

Carter sighed. "I was so wrong about her. The cameras are gone, but if anything, she's worse. I didn't want to believe you. Who wants to accept they've driven someone completely bonkers? She kept calling constantly, coming over at all hours. And that's not the worst part. I called Dave."

"What do you mean?"

"About the roses. I wanted to know why he put that message when he sent them. He hedged a little bit and then admitted Holly told him what to put. That was the favor she wanted from him."

We'll always be friends. She could have chosen a number of meaner things. But she wanted it to sound like Carter, wanted me to believe it was coming from him.

"I asked her about it and she lied and lied to me and then finally broke down and admitted it. And then my phone rang and she realized it was you and grabbed the phone out of my hand and demanded I choose her instead."

"Carter, I'm sorry."

"You have nothing to be sorry for. I was too close to the situation to see it clearly.

When Holly and I were kids, we used to go into each other's

houses without knocking, play kickball in the field down the street. I was with her when she learned how to drive. Holly hit a mailbox during her first lesson and we had to knock on the door and tell the people who lived there. It's a great story. But now all those memories are painful. I was trying to hold onto what we were, but it's gone. We can't be friends when she wants more and I can't give her that. Especially when she went behind my back to try to hurt you."

"So now what?" My heart ached for him, but also felt lighter, knowing he finally saw what the rest of us did.

"Now I'd like to start over. With no cameras and no crazy exes, real or imagined. How does that sound?" I could hear his smile through the phone.

"That sounds great."

***

Carter and I talked every day and we always ended the conversation the same way. He would say, "I love you." And I would reply, "I love you, too. What should we do about it?"

And then we'd hang up. We had issues, and I was okay with it. Because what I hadn't told Carter was that while he was getting his classroom ready for a new year, I was researching jobs and apartments in Minot. Just in case. The only person I'd told was Katelyn. She thought I was nuts. But she couldn't tell me that without a big grin spreading across her face.

She came over to watch the premier of the show with me. I was so jumpy I couldn't sit still.

"Calm down. They'll only be a couple hundred thousand people watching, instead of the millions that would have watched it on NBC."

I poked her in the shoulder. "Thanks, I feel so much better now."

"You look nice. Are we video conferencing with Carter? Is that what your computer is all set up for?"

"Yes. And his family is with him. Yikes, I'm scared. My mom wanted me to watch at her house. She's having a bunch of friends over for a viewing party. You couldn't pay me to join that. But I feel bad that you're meeting him when I haven't even told her he exists."

"Well lucky me. I guess Doug Jr. here better hurry up and finish eating."

Doug Jr. was snorting his way through his meal and did not tolerate nursing cover-ups.

"Doug didn't want to come?" I hoped Katelyn's husband wasn't afraid of offending me. I wanted him to feel welcome.

"Are you kidding? He has all his sports games and commentary taped and he watches as many as he can fit in when I'm not home. He's probably eating those disgusting microwave pizza bites he loves. This is great for him."

"I'm so glad."

"Besides, we have two more weeks before the doctor approves me for, ahem, intimacy, and we are both climbing the walls. I needed to get out of there."

"Oh gross, Katelyn. Way too much info." I wanted to lob a pillow at her and wipe that stupid grin off her face, but I didn't think Doug Jr. would like that very much.

"The struggle is real my friend. The struggle is real." She cackled as I bent over, pretended to barf.

When the baby was satisfied and sleepily settled in Katelyn's lap, I called Carter and held my breath as his face popped up on the screen. Man, he was handsome. He gave me a nervous smile and moved out of the way so I could see his parents and sister waving. I wondered what they thought of all this as I gave them a little wave back.

Carter's mom had his curly blonde hair and dimples, but the rest of his face came from his Dad. They had the same dark blue eyes.

I introduced Katelyn and they all oohed and awed over little Doug Jr. We had ten minutes to kill before the show started and a newborn baby made a convenient icebreaker.

Carter came back to sit in front of the camera and I resisted the urge to stroke my computer. Maybe I'd tell him later and we could laugh about it.

He stared into my eyes. "Don't be nervous." I wasn't sure if he was referring to seeing us on TV or meeting his family.

Katelyn nudged me. "He's cute," she whispered.

Carter's lips twitched, letting me know he'd heard her. It was so much fun seeing all his facial expressions again, but terrible as well, reminding me of our physical distance.

Behind him, Carter's mom and sister stood up and came over to the computer so they could talk to us. Carter's little sister blushed to the roots when Katelyn and I told her how much we liked her music. I asked her what she was working on next and she stopped biting her lip and forgot to be shy as she told us about the songs she planned to record.

Carter's mom beamed and put her arm around her daughter. "She's leaving for college in a few weeks and she has a full-ride scholarship. We couldn't be prouder." She leaned into the computer and whispered, "Carter is so happy lately. You light him up in a way I've never seen before. Plus, you made him ditch Holly, which I thought would never happen."

"Mom!" Carter's sister giggled and glanced behind them see if he could hear us.

"I know it's a terrible thing to say, but Carter's been rescuing Holly from scrapes since elementary school and he usually ended up in the most trouble."

She was about to say something else, but Carter came over with a curious smile and the group of us looked at him with guilty faces.

"Gossiping, I see. I'll leave you to it. But the show is starting after this set of commercials."

"Yes, sir." His mom saluted and gave me a wink before going to sit back on their couch. She squeezed her husband's hand and whispered something in his ear. I liked her already.

Katelyn grabbed my arm as *Real Love* splashed across the screen, followed by a voiceover telling viewers a little bit about the show as the screen filled with images of the unimpressive apartment complex and clips of us doing dishes, cleaning toilets, and doing yard work. They zoomed in on Carter's bare chest a bit longer than necessary and Carter's dad, who I knew from Carter's descriptions to be quiet man, laughed aloud and slapped his knee.

"Son, that's embarrassing."

"Thanks, Dad."

Next came snippets of us reading the packet so viewers would understand the rules of the show. As I'd assumed, they clipped back and forth from the women to the men and went to a commercial break after Holly's bathroom meltdown.

I let out a long breath of air and then rested my elbows on my knees.

"Are you going to watch all the episodes with your family?" I whispered to Carter. He had his computer next to him again.

182

He shook his head. "Only this one. I keep thinking about all the things I don't want them to see, like my country dancing."

"I'm sure they've watched you dance before," I teased.

"Well, yeah, but I don't need to hear them laughing about it. They can do that at their house."

After the commercial break, the show got right into introductions, including Tyson handing me his shirt across the table. The way they edited it, I might as well have demanded it so he could flex for me. So embarrassing.

"Tyson is gorgeous," Carter's sister murmured.

"Not on your life." Carter reached over the couch and ruffled her hair.

I laughed, but then my eyes riveted back to my TV as they showed black and white footage of Michelle and Patrick's fight in our apartment. The sound was bad, but they had captions at the bottom of the screen. And then the TV cut away to interviews where Michelle denied having any feelings for Patrick, before cleverly cutting back to black and white clips of them making out on our couch.

"Carter."

He turned to me with a panicked face. Hidden cameras.

"I bet they're in the gym, too." He gave me a sympathetic look. "They'll show you falling off the treadmill."

"And our first kiss," I added, blushing.

"Oh, how sweet," his mom said, turning her head around to look at Carter.

Not really. Carter picking me up and tossing me out of his apartment? Not the kind of thing we wanted to explain to friends and family.

"You didn't know about the cameras in the apartments?" Katelyn asked.

"I should have." *Stinky Dave.* He wouldn't get away with this. You couldn't record someone without their knowledge in California. They had a news story about it once. I'd find a number for Weston. I didn't know what kind of a lawyer he was, but he was going to help me sue the pants off Dave.

"Do you know Weston's last name?" I asked Carter. They'd been roommates, maybe he'd know. Hopefully it wasn't something common like Smith or Johnson.

"Yeah, it's Vondrasek."

That made things easier.

***

Carter called me as I was getting ready for bed. We'd been on the phone or computer practically all day, but it didn't dim the happiness I felt in hearing from him again.

"You sitting there stewing about the show?"

"I'm trying not to, but it's so weird seeing us on TV. Hey Carter, about our first kiss. When you started avoiding me, was it only about doing what Holly wanted?"

Carter stayed quiet for a moment. "That was part of it, but I also realized I was falling for you and it scared me. I was afraid of losing control of my heart on a TV show. Obviously, my attempts to keep you away didn't work."

I smiled. "Sorry to wreck your plans."

"Speaking of plans, I have some news that should cheer you up."

"Oh really?" I sat down and picked at the old quilt on my bed.

"I'm coming to see you on Saturday."

Joy burst out of me, and excitement and guilt and then worry. "No, I should come see you. Even with no vacation days left, I could come for a weekend."

We weren't supposed to be seen together, but I should have stopped worrying about that and gone to see him weeks ago, before the show started airing. Now being without him seemed unbearable.

"School doesn't start for a few more weeks and I already bought the plane ticket so don't worry about that."

"But I should pay for it, and I hate that you have to get on a plane again."

"You're not paying for it and my sister is coming with me so I'll have a flying buddy. She wants to see her aunt one last time before she leaves for college. You do want me to come, right?"

"Yes! I want you here tonight."

He laughed. "Well, good to know. I love you."

"I love you, too. What should we do about it?"

"We should meet up, Saturday morning."

"It's supposed to be 112 degrees this weekend."

"Sounds perfect."

CHAPTER 28

The next morning, we had what Sherry and Jeffy called a 'Viewing Party on the Radio.' They took questions and comments off of social media, emails and from callers and devoted an hour to me chatting with fans, with occasional traffic and music breaks.

During our prep meeting, Mr. Langley had ordered me to stay away from the comments, especially on Twitter. And while I would have ordinarily balked at walking blindly into a radio interview, I knew why he didn't want me to see them.

After talking to Carter last night, I'd made the mistake of googling my name and *Real Love*. Yowza. I had to remind myself internet trolls did that to everybody and closed the screen. It helped that I had other things to think about. Like Carter coming on Saturday!

After work, I googled Weston and found an office number for him. Thinking I'd have to leave a message or talk to a secretary first, I was not prepared to hear his voice right away.

"Hello, Weston Vondrasek speaking."

"Weston? This is Bethany, Bethany Parks, from the show." I felt dumb adding that on, but I also didn't want an awkward pause while he scrambled to remember me.

"Bethany, baby. So good to hear from you. You see the episode last night? Thinking about me?"

Um, no. "Yeah, about the show, I thought I'd ask since you're a lawyer. Can they get away with the hidden cameras? Isn't it illegal in California to film people without their knowledge?"

"Way ahead of you. I have copies of everything we signed. Hold on, let me find this part I highlighted last night." He hummed the *Mission Impossible* theme while I waited for him to stop shuffling papers.

"Ah, ha. Here it is. 'I understand that I may be filmed at any time, in any common area, excepting bathing and toilet areas, and that I am responsible for my conduct and any action or recourse that may come from anything I say, do, or participate in while being filmed.' So basically, we agreed to it, legally. Morally...yeah, it wasn't very nice. But you know, if you wanted to come into town, have dinner, we could chat about this more. You could stay at my pl—"

"Thanks for the info, Weston."

He chuckled. "Anytime, baby. Anytime."

I hung up, shaking my head. Good ole Weston. He'd been awfully cheerful. The law firm must have welcomed him back.

Dave covered his tracks, that wasn't surprising. And in a small way, I was relieved. Teaming up with Weston on a long shot didn't sound like my idea of fun. I had more important things to do, like cleaning my house, going through outfits (Carter would never see me in gaucho pants again) and deciding whether to introduce Carter to my mom while he was here. With her mom radar, she'd probably sense his presence and hunt us down anyway.

After mopping my floors and changing the sheets in the guest bedroom, I called Carter to find out his flight number and see if I could pick him up from the airport on Saturday, but the call went straight to voicemail. It felt weird to go to bed without talking to him. After a few minutes of tossing and turning, I got up and dug out Michelle's number. Maybe I'd be able to sleep if I put my mind elsewhere, and my conversation with Weston made me curious about how she was handling the first episode. To my surprise, she laughed it off.

"Bethany, I was so paranoid, I could never let my guard down anywhere in that place, even to pee. That was part of the reason we left the show early. If it gives some people a laugh, good for them. I'll always be grateful to Dave for bringing us back together, but he's not getting an invitation to my wedding."

"I don't blame you. Have you set a date yet?"

"No, but give me your address so I can send you an invitation when we do. Would you want me to send one to Carter?" Her voice sounded hesitant, as if afraid I might be offended by the question.

I couldn't help grinning. "Hopefully we'd go together."

She squealed. "Well now you have to tell me everything."

***

Carter called me the next morning, sounding chipper, but tired.

"Did you not sleep well last night?" I asked.

"Oh, I slept fine. Sorry, I was out with some guy friends and my phone died."

I knew Carter well enough to know when he sounded odd, and he did now. *Why couldn't he have borrowed one of his friend's phones to call me?* But I refused to be jaded by my experience with Todd. If Carter said he couldn't call me, he must have had his reasons.

"What airline are you flying? I want to meet you at the airport."

"Um, Delta. But, don't worry about that. I'm going to rent a car and drop my sister at my aunt's first and then come to your place. Is that okay?"

"That's fine. You don't have to rent a car, though. I could drop your sister off, and then we can have more time together. When does your flight come in?"

"Um, hold on, it's Saturday morning, but I don't remember the exact time. I'm driving, I'll have to text all that stuff to you later. Will that work?"

"Yeah." He was acting really weird. "Is everything okay? Carter, if you can't fly here just tell me and I'll come to you. Or if you need more time we can put this off."

Carter sighed. "Oh, Bethany. I can't wait to see you. Trust me, I'm coming. I'm in fast moving traffic that keeps stopping suddenly, but I promise I'll text you all the information. If you want to come to the airport I certainly won't stop you. I love you."

"I love you, too. Drive safe."

I pulled into the work parking lot and sat in my car for a few minutes, tapping my phone on the steering wheel. *Trust Carter. Easier said than done*, the snarky side of my brain countered. The best thing to do was throw myself into work. So I shook out my shoulders, put my phone away and headed inside. I had a great idea for a new contest and I needed to type it all up and research it before presenting it to Mr. Langley.

A text from Carter came right before my lunch hour. **Flight 2471, Delta Airlines, 8:05 a.m.**

I smiled. In less than twenty-four hours, Carter would be here. I started googling restaurants, knowing he loved good Mexican food.

Jeffy walked out of the sound booth, having just finished recording our new jingle. He came over to lean on my desk and see what I was working on.

"Looking for a good place for lunch? I want to come."

"I'm in." Patty joined us after grabbing a sheet from the printer near my desk and glancing at my computer screen. "I can't eat another microwave noodle cup knowing you guys are headed out."

It wouldn't hurt to be more social. And it wasn't like I could tell them the real reason I'd been researching restaurants.

Patty was supposed to take a lunch after mine, but Mr. Langley begrudgingly gave her permission to go with me and we headed outside to Jeffy's car. He claimed to have the best air conditioning. We knew the true motive. He wanted us to see the inside of his Mustang. We obligingly complimented him on his wicked stereo system and custom leather seats.

"So about this guy from the show that you're desperately in love with—"

"Nope." I shook my head. "I'm off the clock. No show questions."

Patty's shoulders slumped. "But I have to know. Is it Tyson or Carter? Or is it Weston? He's my favorite. I like the bad boys."

"Weston's too self-absorbed to be a bad boy." *Dang.* "Change of subject."

Jeffy laughed. "My vote's on Tyson. He looks like the type to love 'em and leave 'em."

As much as I wanted to defend Tyson's honor, I didn't trust my mouth to explain without giving away more than I should. "I'm not pining over anyone from the show. I don't even know how you guys got that idea."

And then my phone rang and Patty saw Carter's name before I could hide it.

"Oh, wow!" She laughed aloud.

I silenced the call and put my phone away. "It's a different Carter."

"Right." Jeffy sighed. "If only I'd been born with a face not made for radio. It's the blond curls and dimples isn't it?"

"You guys cannot say anything. It's in my contract that I can't reveal outcomes. You could get me sued."

Patty's face sobered. "I promise to keep it to myself. But if you wanted to call him back, you don't have to wait until after lunch. We'll plug our ears, won't we Jeffy?"

How kind of them. "Nope. I'm good."

I quickly texted Carter that I was in a lunch meeting and then asked Jeffy more questions about his car as we pulled into the parking lot of the restaurant.

I called Carter back as I was walking out to my car after work.

"Sorry about earlier. A couple of my co-workers went to lunch with me, and I'm not very good with stealth. They know about us."

Carter snickered. "You make it sound like we have something to hide."

"Well we do. People aren't supposed to know we're together until after the show." *Maybe I should rethink those dinner plans.*

"I don't care about any of that and I'm not afraid of Dave. What is he going to do? Sue me for all the money I don't have? Get yourself a pair of those gigantic sunglasses and a floppy hat. I'll do the same. Isn't that how everyone looks there?"

"You're going to hate Arizona, but it will only be for a few days." I grinned. New plan, find places to go with air-conditioning and old people who don't watch reality TV.

"I don't hate Arizona." Carter sounded serious. "I like to tease you about Arizona, but I don't hate it. I would live anywhere to be with you."

I should tell him, I should tell him I'm thinking about moving to Minot. But my fear held me back and then he changed the subject.

Carter made me want to be more open with my feelings, but he also didn't push me to reciprocate. He let me be me. And that was something special. I felt bad for doubting him earlier. *Sometimes it's hard to read people over the phone.*

***

I woke up with the phone in my hand, the alarm blaring, and stared blearily eyed at the time. 7:00 a.m. Hopefully Carter was getting some sleep on the plane. We'd talked until way too late. In fact, I'd tried to hang up several times and Carter kept right on talking while I yawned and complained that we could talk tomorrow and he needed to be up early for his flight. I doubted he'd gotten any sleep at all.

The shower water did not wake me up and I'm pretty sure I dozed off for a couple minutes. Even with skipping breakfast, I dashed out the door in a hurry, checking Carter's flight status after starting my car. ON TIME. Dang it. Too much time spent fixing my hair and makeup.

I sent him a quick text, letting him know I was leaving for the airport and then pulled out of the driveway.

Don't go yet. My flight's delayed.

What? **Are you on the plane?**

You don't need to go to the airport.

I pulled to the side of the road at the end of my neighborhood and stared at my phone. Oh no. Maybe the plane trip was too much for him. Maybe he missed his flight because we talked too late. *I should have gone there. I should have insisted.*

My phone rang and I let out a sigh. I needed to hide my disappointment from him. I'd go there to see him. It was no big deal, except it was.

"Hi Carter. What's going on?"

"Turn around, babe."

"I don't understand."

"I love you. Turn your car around and come back to your house. You told me you drive a green Toyota Corolla, right? Is that you idling down there?"

I checked my rear-view mirror and saw a rental truck with a food trailer attached to the back of it. Pulling up to my house. *No way.*

With shaking hands, I put my car in drive and tried to make a U-turn that turned into an awkward three-point turn. How embarrassing. A giddy laugh escaped as the tears started flowing. I pulled into my driveway and met Carter halfway across the lawn where he picked me up and swung me around.

"Carter." His kiss stopped anything else I might say, and for a minute all I could do was revel in the feel of his arms around me and his lips on mine.

He pulled back and put me down gently, looking me in the eyes with a worried expression.

I touched his scruffy cheek. "Why did you try to make me think you were flying?"

"Well I hoped to ease you in to the idea of me moving here. I know how big expressions of feelings are hard for you. If I'm freaking you out and you need some space, I'll leave you alone. I promise. It's a big city and I'll work through the school year and then head back to Minot. But I already quit my job there after I got an offer here so it's—" I grabbed his shirt front and silenced him with my lips, doing my best to convince him that he had nothing to worry about.

He rubbed his unshaven face against my neck, murmuring, "Bethany, being away from you drove me crazy. A little vacation wouldn't be enough."

I smiled. "I would have moved to Minot."

"Maybe in a few years." He grinned at me and searched my eyes, looking for panic. "For now, I could use a shower and a nap. The moving truck broke down. I had to drive all night to get here in time. And then I'd love it if you'd help me search for an apartment."

"Sounds like a plan."

My heart felt so full I thought it might burst. Taking Carter's hand, I led him into my house and the rest of our lives together. And maybe I'd take the next bold move and propose first.

EPILOGUE

"Daddy, daddy!"

Lizzie threw her arms around Carter as he walked in the door. I was looking forward to my own greeting, but I held back so he could hug his little girl.

"Elizabeth Bernice Allred. How's my favorite daughter doing?" Carter's blue eyes twinkled as he picked her up and twirled her around.

"Dad," Lizzie said, giggling. "I'm your only daughter."

Carter kissed her nose and put her back on her feet. She grabbed his hand and brought him over to the kitchen table where her friend sat coloring a picture.

"This is Kendra, but she doesn't want a hug."

"Okay," Carter said, trying to keep a straight face. "Nice to meet you Kendra."

"Dad, I drawed you a picture." Lizzie upended the stack, searching for the one she'd colored for him.

I'd turned back toward the dishes in the sink, but felt Carter's hands come around me and his lips tickling my ear. "What, no hug from you either?"

I whirled around and kissed him, sighing in delight. After nine years of marriage, he could still send a thrill right through me with a simple look.

"Your middle name's Bernice?" Lizzie's friend asked.

"Dad says I'm named after a car. But Mom says I'm named after a doll. They're so weird."

Carter laughed and whispered in my ear, "When she's sixteen and she hates us for it, I'm telling her it was your idea."

"Like she'd believe that." I turned his face back towards my lips and gave him another kiss, not meaning to let it linger too long. We had company after all.

"Ewww. Stop kissing! So gross." Lizzie pushed between us and held up the picture she'd been looking for. "I found it Daddy. This is for you."

Taking her hand, Carter made a big production of finding a place for it on the fridge. Then he came back to help me with the dishes.

"How was the first day?" I asked.

Carter grinned. "Seventh grade choir will always be my favorite. The boys are trying to impress each other with armpit farts. They're all shorter than the girls and their voices can't stay on pitch while they're talking, let alone singing. No one can sit still and the girls constantly roll their eyes. They think everything is lame, especially me."

I laughed. "And they're your favorite?"

"By the end of the year they almost resemble a real choir. I like the challenge." He handed me a plate to put in the dishwasher. "What about you? Did you get any work done with lil miss and her friend here?"

"Some. I finished the press releases that were due today. Lizzie starts kindergarten next week. Can you believe it?"

His shoulders slumped. "It went by so fast. She's still my baby." He glanced at our daughter and then back at me. "Are you thinking of going back to the office? Or do you want to continue working from home?"

My face flushed hot and I had to look away. I'd been planning on finding a cute way to tell him, but I had never been good at keeping secrets.

"What's wrong, babe?" He took a wet bowl out of the sudsy water, his eyebrows wrinkling in concern. "I know it's hard to think of her growing up."

Best to get it out. "We're pregnant."

The bowl slipped from his fingers and smashed on the tile. *Darn, that was from our wedding set. I knew I should have told him with balloons or something.*

The girls ran over to see the mess and Carter shooed them

back, but he had the silliest grin on his face and it melted my heart. We'd reached the point where one kid was all we thought we'd get.

He leaned over the pieces on the floor and kissed my cheek. "Sorry about the bowl. You excited?"

"Excited, nervous, freaked out. You know me."

I got out the broom from the side of the fridge and Carter reached for it. "I'll take care of this. You should sit down. How are you feeling, sick at all?"

"Carter." I bent down to get the big pieces in the garbage so he could sweep the rest. "I'm the same as I was a minute ago. Pregnant, and very much in love with you."

He raised an eyebrow. "Are you sure?"

"Am I sure I love you? Yes."

"No. I know you love me, goof. Are you sure you don't need a rest?" After dumping the broken shards in the garbage, he put the broom and dust pan away. Then he turned to study me again.

"Don't worry. I'll take a rest right after we get Lizzie off to bed. We'll snuggle on the couch and if you want to kiss me or get handsy, no one will tell you, 'cut it out,' or 'ew,' not even me." I'd wanted to keep a straight face as I said it, but I broke down and started giggling.

Carter tried to look stern, but his eyes gave him away. "We both know you're the handsy one. I'm an innocent bystander."

Rolling my eyes, I turned the water back on to finish the dishes and a hand slapped my bum. *I rest my case.*

33595802R00112

Made in the USA
San Bernardino, CA
06 May 2016